THE
YEAR OF
SILENCE

BOOKS BY
MADISON SMARTT BELL

THE WASHINGTON SQUARE ENSEMBLE

WAITING FOR THE END OF THE WORLD

STRAIGHT CUT

ZERO DB AND OTHER STORIES

THE YEAR OF SILENCE

THE
YEAR OF
SILENCE

MADISON
SMARTT
BELL

TICKNOR & FIELDS
NEW YORK
1987

COPYRIGHT © 1987 by Madison Smartt Bell

All rights reserved. No part of this work may be reproduced or transmitted in any form or by any means, electronic or mechanical, including photocopying and recording, or by any information storage or retrieval system, except as may be expressly permitted by the 1976 Copyright Act or in writing from the publisher. Requests for permission should be addressed in writing to Ticknor & Fields, 52 Vanderbilt Avenue, New York, New York 10017.

LIBRARY OF CONGRESS CATALOGING-IN-PUBLICATION DATA

Bell, Madison Smartt.
  The year of silence.

  I. Title.
PS3552.E517Y4 1987   813'.54   86-30189
ISBN 0-89919-490-7

PRINTED IN THE UNITED STATES OF AMERICA

P 10 9 8 7 6 5 4 3 2 1

To the memory of the dead
and the hope of the living

Il faut imaginer Sisyphe heureux.

Albert Camus,
Le Mythe de Sisyphe

THE
YEAR OF
SILENCE

THE
YEAR OF
SILENCE

EVERY WEEKDAY MORNING after Weber left for school Tom Larkin would set up the practice board; that was the first thing he did when he got out of bed. He could sleep later than Weber, who had to rise at six in order to get up-town in time for his eight o'clock bell, but most mornings he was awake as early just the same, lying in his small cubicle listening to the shuffle of Weber's preparations until the door clicked shut behind him. It was a very small apartment but Weber had arrived at some sense of space by keeping the living room stripped virtually bare. The practice board had folding legs that Larkin had appropriated from a card table and sawed off to the proper height, and he kept it stored in a closet when it was not in use. After he set up the board he posed a chair in front of it and then left the room, to make coffee or take a shower or sometimes only to create a pause, an interval during which he would remind himself again that faith might indeed move mountains. After this he would return to the front room, hesitating for a half beat on the threshold like someone preparing for a leap, then cross the floor as if crossing a stage and sit down and begin.

He had made the practice board himself, though ordinarily he had little skill with such things, digging out the edges of each key with a gutter-shaped sculptor's instrument he had borrowed and then smoothing out the edges with a little rasp. He'd blackened all the sharps and flats with shoe polish and left the others unstained; by now their light pine color had deepened and taken on a patina from the oils of his hands. It was a standard keyboard, with nothing lacking but the body of the instrument, flexion of the keys, and sound.

Because it was the least inconvenient spot, Larkin set up the practice board against the row of long mirrors Weber had attached to the apartment's single unencumbered wall. Weber was a fanatic practitioner of some kind of karate, and daily upon his return from the high school where he taught he would perform its crisp movements before the rank of mirrors, installed not for the sake of vanity but simply to correct mistakes. Under ordinary circumstances Weber was graceless and frequently bumped into things, but he had an attitude toward his own flesh which Larkin had known elsewhere only among dancers: a divorcement of the body from any sense of self, a dispassionate regard of it as the material of which the work is to be made. The force of his concentration hung around the room like an aura, mingling no doubt with whatever humors Larkin's own exertions could raise.

Every morning of every working day he applied himself to the cool architectonics of the Goldberg Variations, the centerpiece of the recital he was due to give at Alice Tully

Hall in roughly three months' time. He played methodically, fingers slapping against the divisions of the plank with rigor, facing himself in the mirrors. His face was round and dark, a little owlish, and otherwise unremarkable and unmemorable by his own private judgment. His expression rarely changed at all during his long practice sessions; always it was tranquil and detached, though he had things to think about that might well have made him writhe. The Lincoln Center debut was the break of his career, would very likely determine whether he would have a real career or not, and it was just one whisker short of certifiable insanity to prepare for it by practicing on an immobile block of wood.

Conceivably there was a strain of madness running in his family. That was a notion which frequently occurred to him while his hands worked contrapuntally up and down the keyboard: he might be prone to whatever germ of craziness had turned his older brother into a hermit and finally, it would seem, had dropped him off the face of the earth. It had been just slightly over a year since Clarence Larkin had vanished altogether out of the Brooklyn slum in which he was reported to be living. The disappearance had brought Tom Larkin home from Europe, where he'd been studying after a tour. At first he'd hoped to find his brother alive and well, but later even discovering a body would have been a comfort.

In the second month, when the search was flagging, when the officials involved had completely lost interest and his parents had subsided into a dreary lack of further expectation, Larkin had decided to take a vow. The idea was so completely unlike him and sufficiently like his brother to be quite appropriate for the circumstances. Nominally, the intention was to purchase his brother's return at the price of his own mortification, though in his rational mind Larkin never believed that it would work. But at the worst it would provide his own uncertainty with a terminal point. When the year was out he could play the piano again and begin to grieve.

Until then, practice meant the rap-tap of his finger ends on pine. The Lincoln Center engagement had come up after the vow was in effect and Larkin did not believe it was enough excuse to break it. By a coincidence of dates he would have two weeks to practice on a sounding keyboard. Of course that was hardly enough time to accomplish anything much. But meanwhile, the fingering was everything, wasn't it? Larkin's face remained solemn and remote in the mirror, betraying no hint of the lunatic laughter that rocked him within. He was a fool, there was no doubt about it, but lately he had discovered that he enjoyed being a fool and that it gave him a sense of contentment unknown to him before he had become one.

Last year he had had a music teacher, a stern old German, blocky and bald as a brick wall, who had finally told him in a fit of temper that he would never be a great concert performer because he liked music too much. "You like listening to yourself," the old man had said, "and that's nothing but a distraction. It's not *your* job to enjoy it."

Larkin paused at the end of the slow twenty-fifth variation and wiped a trace of sweat from his temples and his upper lip. *I hope you're satisfied now*, he thought at his teacher. *It's hard to imagine enjoying this.*

He resumed playing, his fingertips traveling through intricate interlocking patterns on the keys. There was no harm in foolishness, he believed, but the prospect of madness worried him a little. He had heard no music for almost as long as he'd stopped playing, only a Janis Joplin grab-bag tape that Weber liked to play over and over, and occasionally someone's boom box passing by on the street outside. No real music — listening made him want to play, a desire he already had trouble enough suppressing. But almost every morning of late, during the gap he always contrived between setting up the board and sitting down before it, he caught himself in the expectation that when he began to practice today each note would sound aloud.

And *that* was truly crazy.

Larkin played on, looking vaguely past his reflection in the mirror. He had all thirty variations down by heart and needed no sheet music. From the windows behind him came the rush of tires over pavement, ceasing and beginning again. A car door banged and a voice called out something indistinct, followed by a long sharp whistle. Farther away a musical klaxon reiterated the opening bar of "La Cucaracha." Someone was clumping slowly up the stairwell of the building, pausing now and again to rest. In Weber's kitchen the hot water tap was irregularly dripping. Larkin's hands raced over the keyboard, each movement dislodging a minute chip of silence. Silent and invisible, delicately balanced as a card house, an unheard music of the mind rose all around him.

In the dark of his little room Larkin lay staring up at where his ceiling was. In Weber's room across the hall a pair of guitars screeched to a halt and Joplin began to squall out the first verse of "Ball and Chain." Weber had been fixed on this particular tape ever since Larkin had moved in. He frequently asked Larkin if it disturbed him, and Larkin always said that it did not, which was the truth.

A chink of light from a street lamp below stood in the

highest corner of the room, which had little floor space but a rather high ceiling, so that it resembled nothing so much as an absurdly deep coffin, or so Larkin sometimes thought. His mattress covered the floor entirely, lapping from baseboard to baseboard, and in the morning he had to fold it back in order to open the door. There was a lamp clipped to the window ledge and a closet, and that was all. However, Larkin paid only about a fourth of Weber's rent and he couldn't afford much better quarters anywhere. The height of the ceiling was sufficient to keep claustrophobia at bay and the wedge of light which hung on the wall gave him something to look at through the long nights when he could not sleep. He had that and Janis Joplin, muted through the two closed doors, for company.

Weber had been a bit queer for just about a year now, ever since his girlfriend had died in unlucky circumstances of one kind or another. Larkin knew little about it because he'd been in Europe for quite a long time and hadn't known the woman. Weber was a friend from college and Larkin hadn't found him obviously changed on his return, only a little more taciturn than before, more moody. It was thought by several other friends, however, that Weber would be better off not living alone, and he himself had offered the compartment with its low rent at a time when Larkin would have done almost anything to get out of the gathered gloom of his parents' house. They'd proved compatible enough, though each tended to go his separate way.

Except for the Janis Joplin fetish Weber was much the same as ever: quiet and almost suspiciously controlled. But he'd developed a rather curious drinking pattern. About one night a week he'd come in with a pint of vodka which he'd ceremoniously offer first to Larkin, who did not drink at all because his brother had. Then Weber would drink most of the vodka himself, rapidly but with apparent distaste, like an unpleasant medicine self-administered. He drank out of a little glass, tilting his head to one side like a bird. The vodka was always a cue for a long loud night of Joplin, after Weber had disappeared behind his own door, and by now Larkin had memorized every pulse and gesture of the tape, the awkward grinding drive of the guitars and keyboards and that voice strained to the breaking point and beyond it.

They were always a little off-beat and a little off-key but the music had grown on him and he had a taste for it now, notwithstanding the endless repetitions. At the worst it was something to fill up the insomniac nights. Since the new year he had slept very badly and now they were well into March. It was a devil's choice because if he did sleep he had long tortured nightmares in which he followed his brother toward some catastrophe or other, often merging identities with him, in the way of dreams. Without sleep he became disoriented and the hours of practice were a hardship to get through. Also, he had begun to hear voices when he lay awake in his little room, though they didn't have much to say to him, only, sometimes, his name. Joplin's ravings would at least drive those to ground and for that Larkin was grateful.

The Goldberg Variations had originally been written to beguile sleep, and Baron von Kayserling had rewarded Bach with a hundred pieces of gold for the work. Larkin might have paid as much for a night without dreams or voices, supposing he had had it. But he had begun to think of it as a bloodless piece of music, for all its manifold beauties, and played in silence it made a very thin diet indeed. Larkin looked up at the light on the wall. Tonight was the night of the two hundred and eighty-sixth day; seventy-nine were left to go. Swollen with the headlights of a passing car, the scrap of light raced all around the upper edges of the room and then returned to its original position. It hung there under Larkin's scrutiny through all the watches of night and withered and began to fade out into the first morning of the spring.

"Sleep well?" Weber said. He was sitting at a little end table pushed against the kitchen window, contemplating two fried eggs on a plate before him. A grammar text and a grade book lay on the table at his elbow.

"Fine," Larkin said. Their household harmony was founded on such courteous lies as this. He edged around the corner of the table into the kitchen and tilted the espresso pot from the stove to check its contents. Half a cup, cooling. The first taste of the coffee set his head spinning, reminding him how badly he was starved for sleep.

"Aren't you running a little late, Weber?"

"I called in sick." Silhouetted against the window, Weber's arm rose and fell, working his fork. Sunlight from the window glared all around his form, so that his edges seemed to shimmer. Blinking, Larkin went to the corner of the table and sat with his back to the light.

"A nice day, too," Weber said brightly. He reached behind him and set his plate down on the edge of the sink and scooted his chair out from the table.

Larkin closed his eyes and opened them again. A current of lively air ran in under the raised sash of the window; Weber was right, it was a nice day. Larkin looked at him. He seemed weirdly chipper, though the rims of his eyes were red. Larkin checked the trash can at his feet and spotted the Smirnoff pint on the top; he'd got through the whole thing this time.

Weber drummed his fingers on the edge of the table and then withdrew his hands to his belt.

"Too pretty a day to just sit around," he said. "I'm going for a walk, I think, up on the bridge maybe. You want to go?"

Larkin wagged his head, heavy as a wrecking ball. "Don't think I'm quite awake yet," he said. "I might follow you . . ."

"Sure," Weber said. "See you." He stood up and picked up his jacket from the floor of the front room and went out.

Outside, the steady chatter and bustle of people in the street went on, and underneath it an incongruous twittering of birds. It had been some time, Larkin thought, since he had noticed birdsong. As much as anything else the sounds and the way they carried were a sign of spring. Then there was the curious new feel of the air; it was still cool but the chill was off it, and it was charged with metamorphic possibility.

Larkin spread his fingers and let the draft coming across the windowsill play over them. His elbow brushed his cup and knocked it over and he sat there for a moment watching the milky coffee purl over the rim of the cup onto the waxy surface of the table, creeping toward Weber's school books. *No, I'm not in the best of shape*, he thought. A rivulet approached the edge of the table and with a forced burst of energy he got up and snatched a paper towel and cleaned up all the mess. Then he went into the front room, wavered, and plopped down on a cushion underneath the row of windows there.

Normally Larkin observed weekends and didn't practice Saturday or Sunday, unless maybe he felt like it or there was nothing else to do. Though it was only Friday, Weber's taking the day off made him a little envious. He looked across the room to the mirrors, but his eyes had come unfocused from fatigue and reported his image back only as a blur, some dark shape crouching there on the floor. Going back to bed would never work, but sometimes he'd been able to fool himself asleep, sitting here or even in a kitchen chair. He shut his eyes and let sleep suck at him, a darkening whirlpool.

. . . Larkin . . .

The voice came wrapped in a swishing sound, like the ocean heard in a seashell. Larkin started onto his feet and looked all around himself, his heart pounding in an unhealthy way. Little gold dots hummed around the edges of his vision and he shook his head to clear it. A walk might not be such a bad plan after all. He put on a sweater and found his keys and went out.

Half a block down Eldridge Street from the building, he turned east on Delancey. The weather was fine and fresh and inspiriting. He bought a coffee through the take-out window of a little coffee shop and drank from it as he walked along, beginning to feel considerably more lucid. From Orchard Street on east the Spanish stores spilled out over the sidewalk with bins of bargain clothes and gewgaws. Amidst the crowd ahead of him Larkin saw Weber standing with his bony wrists crossed in front of him, staring openmouthed into the window of a discount electronics store. Larkin came nearer without changing his pace and Weber turned away without seeing him and went on.

Weber was taller than most of the people clogging the sidewalk and so was easy enough to keep in sight. Larkin could see the back of his head and the thick collar of his bomber jacket going along above the heads of others, jerkily, for Weber always had difficulty inserting himself into the flow of pedestrian traffic. In this he was unlike Larkin, who moved with an easy catlike smoothness through the interstices among other passersby; it was one of the few qualities he had shared with his brother.

At Essex Street the sidewalk traffic evaporated quickly and Larkin saw Weber break free of it, wriggling his shoulders and walking down to the next corner with a long loping stride. He crossed to the median of Delancey, paused there to wait for the light. Larkin stopped in the shadow of a newsstand and stood looking vacantly over rows of shining bare flesh aligned on the covers of the slick magazines. He could have overtaken Weber with no trouble, but did not especially want to. He was not in the mood for conversation, after all; he and Weber were aware of each other's polar obsessions but did not discuss them, and under such a weight the exchange of trivialities could be maddening at times. From the corner of his eye he saw Weber cross the street and enter the stairway to the bridge. Larkin waited a few minutes more, finishing his coffee, skimming headlines. Then he crumpled his cup and tossed it in a wastebasket near the newsstand and dawdled along toward the stairs himself.

Distant, indistinct, fantastic, the towers of the bridge ran together with the colors of the sky: blue-gray, gray-blue. It was perfectly clear and the sky was bright but its color was uncertain. Just the elevation of the stairway to the pedestrian ramp was enough to make Larkin feel enlightened, as if he had come up above the world. He went slowly along the slope of the concrete slab that rose gently over the streets and buildings toward a hovering point above the riverbank where the steel superstructure began. Ahead of him three dark dot-sized figures toiled along and up; one of them undoubtedly was Weber. As he watched all three of them slipped between the vertical poles that marked the final arch of the bridge.

By the time Larkin himself reached the main frame there was no one left in sight ahead. He went through the poles into the forest of complicated shadows cast by the girders crisscrossing above. Walking from one patch of sunlight to the next, he approached the center of the span. Somewhere just short of it he stopped and propped his elbows on the rusty tubular rail and looked out. The water below was an uneasy green and a tugboat shoving up the river cut a cream-colored wake along its surface. Two fat white gulls sailed lazily around the tug and Larkin looked down on their backs. To his left the forms of the city were chiseled out with sharp hard glittering sunlight. It was colder on the bridge, though the taste of the air remained pleasant, and the wind dragged Larkin's shortish hair out from his head and sliced through the weave of his sweater. He turned and put his back to it, leaning against the rail.

A measured thumping started up, not quite a sound at first but more a sensation in the soles of his feet, and Larkin looked toward the Brooklyn side. A heavyset Hispanic man came jogging out of the shadows. He wore sweat pants and Nikes and a T-shirt cut off short to expose his belly. As he came nearer, Larkin could distinctly hear his feet hitting the curved metal plates of the walkway in a series of muted rings. He shifted to the opposite rail to pass Larkin with maximum clearance but did not otherwise acknowledge his presence. Larkin followed him with an eye as he ran down the grade toward Manhattan, and the sound of his footfalls was swallowed up in the racket of an approaching train. Banded and ringed with graffiti, the train rushed up to Larkin and began to pass before him. The sound of it was gigantic and all-encompassing; there were dozens of little lines and progressions within it that held Larkin rapt and awed, though it was impossible to follow them all. The train went by him, pulling its tunnel of sound in after it, and Larkin pushed himself off the railing and walked on in the same direction.

At the eastern end of the bridge's span the walkway cut to the right and then back down. As Larkin came into one end of the turn there was someone else coming into the other, a massive man in a long black coat with a scarlet muffler wound around its collar. He had a black beard that started just under his eye sockets and long thick hair that fell to mingle with the fringes of the scarf, and when he saw Larkin he gave a start as if Larkin were something entirely unlikely. After he had passed he turned and looked again, a long incredulous glare, then shook his head and went on up into the higher reaches of the bridge.

Larkin had stopped himself, to make what he could of this encounter: not much. Some way ahead of him a walled concrete ramp sank between the two lanes of highway to the level of the street. The ramp was empty except for some trash and Larkin wondered where Weber had got to; it was not usual for him to go all the way to the Brooklyn side. Certainly he hadn't passed him along the way . . . Larkin dismissed the thought and went a little farther down to where a little square turret stood out from the walk. The building was shut with a padlock on its battered door and there was a balcony running around it, with a small spiral stair that went inexplicably down to the highway. Larkin walked around to the far side of the balcony and stood there, looking out over the north side of Brooklyn. The sky was shading toward a darker gray and it had grown even colder. Larkin stood with his hands gripping the rail and let the wind whip him until he was numb.

In the area spread below him his brother had had his last address, and during the first weeks following his return from Europe Larkin had quartered and combed the neighborhoods, but he hadn't turned up much. The rooms where his brother had lived gave up no implication and neighbors and acquaintances were not much more forthcoming. It appeared that the missing man had lived as anonymous as a shadow. From his post on the turret ledge Larkin could see the comings and goings of people in the streets and at first that brought him back the hunter's sense of alert anticipation that he'd had the first days of his private search, when there had still been hope.

But by now he understood with a dull sense of finality that his brother was no longer in the world. His vow of silence had ceased to be a proffered good in a possible bargain and had become a monument. Down on the streets the people shuttled backward and forward, insectlike, lacking clear identity, and Larkin conceived without bitterness or even sorrow how his brother's life must have broken down into its elemental particles and blown across the people and the place itself like ash. In this thought he could recognize the beginning of resignation and he harbored it with no special emotion, standing motionless for a long time with his fingers frozen to the rail while the wind blew him through the numbness into cold again.

Later he began to realize that the pattern of movement on the streets had changed. People were coagulating, clumping together on street corners. They looked up, shading their eyes, in the direction of the bridge. Noting this, Larkin suspected for a moment that he might be the object of scrutiny himself, as if the mass of people had been reading his mind and chosen to take an interest in its contents. Once the doubtfulness of that bore in on him he turned and craned his neck to follow the direction of the others' regard.

High on the nearest tower of the bridge he saw two silhouettes punched out of the light of the sky. One stood entirely still while the other crept slowly forward to join it, moving almost as imperceptibly as the minute hand of a clock. Larkin grasped that he must be watching a suicide in the process of being foiled, but it was hard to accept the event as real when its actors looked so small, like stick figures a bored child might sketch in the margin of a book. The two had almost touched each other, not quite, when the stationary one broke away in a set of neat evasive movements, a version of what Weber repeated over and over in his living room, only here in miniature.

Larkin jogged back up the walkway to where the main cables sweeping down from the tower crossed it. There was a policeman there, standing next to a three-wheeled scooter, speaking into a hand radio. Two Puerto Rican boys stood at a little distance watching him, one holding the frame of an old bicycle. There was not enough traffic over the walkway for much more of a crowd to have gathered.

"Stand clear," the cop said shortly, as Larkin came up to

the rail, and turned back to his radio. He had on a cap with a long bill instead of the usual hat, Larkin noticed, but otherwise wore ordinary policeman's garb.

"Sorry," Larkin said. "I think maybe I know him . . ." He swept his hand up as if tossing something into the air. The policeman swung toward him, cupping the box of the radio to his face.

"What? How? You saw him go up?" He squinted at Larkin from under the bill of his cap.

"Yes, ah." Larkin, seeing potential weakness in his line of discourse, began to lie. "We'd gone over the bridge together and got separated. I saw him going up the cable from the Brooklyn side."

"So," the policeman said. The radio crackled and he muttered some words of reply and then looked back at Larkin.

"Is he crazy? Ever suicidal before? Could he be armed?"

"No," Larkin said. "Not armed, anyway. He was all right this morning . . . I might be able to talk him down from there," he said. "If you're having problems."

"Yeah," the policeman said. "We are definitely having problems with this guy." He conferred again with the radio. "What's your relationship?"

Larkin hesitated.

"Roommate," he said. "We're old friends."

"All right, then," the cop said. "You can go on up. I mean, I'm not gonna stop you. Be careful, it's windy up there, you fall at your own risk, okay?"

The wide curve of the cable was not a reassuring surface to walk on and Larkin's shoes didn't seem to fit it well. A light wound wire ran waist-high on either side as a support but it gave Larkin little feeling of security, and the whole operation felt altogether too much like a balancing act. He went up the bellying sag of the cable at as steady a pace as he could force, clutching the side rails and looking only at where he set his feet. From time to time a diminished snatch of river or roadway would appear to one side or the other of the cable to send his head wheeling off into vertigo.

He had made it about two-thirds of the way to the top when the wind picked up and he felt the cable groaning and shifting under his feet. He stopped dead still, fingers clamped around the side rails, eyes slammed shut. He waited for the motion to subside but it did not, and after a minute he incautiously opened his eyes to see the eternity of air and space all around him and almost fell then from fright alone. When after some time he had got control of himself again, he fixed his sight on one square inch of the bluish pipe in front of him and advanced.

"Hey, you made it."

Larkin stopped and raised his head. The tower was just before him now, blocking out the terrifying sky. Three officers in windbreakers leaned recklessly back on the side rail just below the point where the cable passed through the side of the tower.

"You the roommate?" said one.

Larkin nodded. The last cop on the row turned toward the tower wall and shouted. "Hey, *buddy*, your friend's coming up now."

No answer returned, only the high whistling of wind through the stanchions continued.

"He's being a little difficult, your pal there," said the officer who had first spoken. "Well, let's see if you have better luck. Come on here and we'll give you a leg up."

There was a three- or four-foot gap between the cable

and the flat top of the tower, which at ground level would have been easy enough to vault, but up here it was a desperate clinging affair. Larkin clawed his way over the edge, keeping his head tucked in. Below, two policemen gripped him at the knee and hoisted. Larkin lifted his eyes in a rash attempt to locate Weber and met again the fearful emptiness of midair. Trembling, he dropped his eyes to the gritty surface of the metal floor and slithered all the way over the top. For a moment he lay at full length in a sort of pushup position, and then he sat up cross-legged, looking down at the space between his knees.

"Well, Tom, decided to come out after all?" Weber said. "It is a nice day, don't you think?"

"Freaking wonderful," Larkin said. He glanced up very briefly in the direction of the voice. Weber stood with his legs set wide near the farther edge of the tower. Larkin could see a portion of the Brooklyn Bridge between his knees. "Come in from the edge there a little, would you?" he said. "You're making me kind of nervous."

"Everybody seems to be taking this the wrong way," Weber said, opening his hands in a gesture of frankness. "It's not what everyone seems to think."

"You're not contemplating the famous dive, then?"

"Never." Weber smiled. "Not even a little bit."

"Then *get away from the edge*, for God's sake."

Weber took several steps in Larkin's direction. "Ah, you've got height fright, haven't you?" he said. "That's too bad."

"So you noticed," Larkin said, looking up again. But planted solidly on the metal plates he felt a good deal safer. "It's not bad as long as I don't have to move."

"The thing is not to look down," Weber said.

"It's not looking down that gets me so much," Larkin said. "It's looking out. I just don't like the way there's nothing there."

"Interesting," Weber said.

"I gather none of this bothers you?"

"No," Weber said. "Not really."

Larkin unfolded his hands palms-up on his knees and saw they had turned black from touching parts of the bridge.

"What did you want to come up here for?" he said.

"Oh, I don't know." Weber shrugged and turned his head south toward the other bridges in the distance. "A change of perspective. You might say I was observing an occasion . . . Look, I would never commit suicide. It's not in my nature. I affirm life." Weber laughed, a little wildly, and tossed back his head. "*I affirm life!*"

"That's terrific," Larkin said. "Only I think they're going to make yours kind of hard for you if you keep on affirming it in this particular way."

"You could be right about that, I suppose."

"It does look a little peculiar, you know."

"Maybe so," Weber said. "So might some of the things you do."

"You have a point." Larkin considered himself momentarily as from Weber's point of view. The whole routine with the practice board might seem a little bizarre to an observer, though not as flamboyantly so as this. He began to chuckle softly. "At least I do it all in the privacy of the home."

"Think it's the same?" Weber squatted down on his heels and knocked the metal in front of him with his knuckles. "Maybe it is, at that. Ever since Marian died I've felt like I've been hauling some kind of weight around all the time.

Oh, I didn't feel guilty or anything. I always understood it wasn't my fault. You might understand what I'm saying here, with your brother dropping out of sight and all."

"Possibly," Larkin said. "You've never said much about her, remember."

Weber shrugged. "It was never really something to talk about. It's an invisible thing, you know, it's just" — he grinned complicitously — "just like a ball and chain."

Joplin roared out sudden and loud in Larkin's inner ear. *Whoawhoawowowowoahahhh* . . .

"What good does it do you to drag it up here?"

"Ah, I don't know," Weber said. "Just shake, rattle and roll, I guess. Maybe none. I hadn't counted on all these cops and things."

"We probably ought to go down," Larkin said.

"All right," Weber said, standing up. His eyes were tired and sagging. "I suppose we'd better."

"One thing," Larkin said. "No one told me anything about it, but I expect you're going to get a little bit arrested here."

"Really," Weber said. "For what? It never was a suicide, after all."

"Trespassing or something," Larkin said. "It probably won't be much."

"I suppose that would follow," Weber said.

"Do me a favor," Larkin said. "Don't put up a big fuss if they do. If you start to rock and roll on that cable somebody's going to get hurt."

"Undoubtedly," Weber said.

"Well?"

"Oh, you've got it," Weber said. "Honor bright."

He walked in the direction of the cable, passing Larkin,

who stood up carefully and went after him. With the flat of the tower under him he felt steady enough even looking over Weber's shoulder, over the edge.

"Well, here we go," one of the cops said. "Need a hand down, anybody?" Two pairs of arms stretched out. Weber hopped down and was received. They accomplished the handcuffing so smoothly that Larkin didn't see them start until they were already finished. Weber crouched and twisted, looking back up at the tower.

"Take it easy, now," Larkin said, and gradually Weber straightened and relaxed.

It was a definite comfort to be on solid pavement again, though down had been a little easier than up; he'd had Weber's back to fix his eyes on all the way. Larkin walked back across Delancey Street toward Weber's building. It was a little past noon, he thought, and with the nervous energy of the climb dissipated he was as frayed and exhausted as he'd been when he got up. At the same coffee shop he'd sampled earlier he stopped and bought a cruller and carried it out onto the street to eat.

Gridlock was setting in along the intersections of Delancey Street all the way back to the bridge, and there was a terrible groaning and wailing of traffic. The heavy blanket of sound came and went from Larkin's ears as his attention started up and failed. He leaned against the wall of the coffee shop with the white paper sack warm in his hand and allowed the people passing on the street to pull his notice to and fro. There was, after all, nothing so unusual about what had been happening, and certainly nothing on the street had been changed by it in the least. Or possibly it was that the extraordinary mixed and blended so thoroughly with the

ordinary that it could not be distinguished in the end. Larkin
dipped a hand into the bag and took the cruller out and bit
it. His eye caught the crimson shirt tail of a girl prancing by
on long high heels and followed the rag of color down to
the corner, where the girl sidestepped out of the path of a
wino shuffling the opposite way.

The wino argued with himself as he crept along, hands
working in curt abortive gestures. He tripped continually
on the long tail of his coat. Larkin watched him, chewing
at his bite of cruller. It came apart into gritty crumbs in his
mouth; there was no savor to it and he could barely get it
down. When he had managed to swallow the mouthful he
looked at the torn end of the pastry, searching it for some
explanation of its uselessness. The wino was now near
enough that snatches of his private conversation were audi-
ble, and Larkin dropped the cruller back in the bag and
rolled the top and handed the package to the wino as he
struggled past. Then he walked on around the corner to
Weber's building and went up.

Everything was as it had been left, only the passing hours
had rearranged all the shadows in the room. Weber was no
longer out for a walk; he was being "observed" overnight
at Bellevue. Larkin went to the closet and dragged out the
practice board and unfolded its legs with a creak and snap.
He flipped it upright and adjusted it before the mirrors and
went into the kitchen, where for a brief distraction he
cleaned the coffee pot and Weber's skillet and plate. With
scouring powder and a rag he scrubbed the black bridge
grime off his hands. As he finished, a roller of dizziness
passed over him, an echo of what he had felt on the bridge,
so that he had to grip the edges of the sink for support.
When the feeling had gone away his head felt empty and

clean, and he went to sit down before the practice board, took a long breath, and began to strike the keys.

In his extreme weariness Larkin was caught up in the mood of the music, for all that no sound came. Its order was itself a kind of passion. He worked at the board with what he felt certain was a greater precision than ever before; his timing had never been better. Confidence gathered in him as he climbed through the variations. There was fervor and wonder in what he was doing, but he no longer felt peculiar about doing it, as he had for the past several months; in the end it was an ordinary thing.

At ease then, Larkin accomplished the lingering twenty-fifth, the climax of the minor variations. During the long rest at the end of it he heard what he'd been half consciously waiting for: a cascade of notes tumbling out into the air, real sound complete with its declining echo. He let the pause hang longer. It was an illusion, sure enough, compounded of his fatigue and the tingling in his fingertips, the latter a tactile reminiscence of the plucked clusters of a harpsichord. Unshaken, he commenced the first of the five final variations, sensing the music in all its particulars as it came carved out of its own deepest silence. Hovering in the mirrors, his face was solemn and unrevealing, though his entire inner self stretched out into a smile. With perfect contentment he realized that he would never play this piece so well again as now. This rendering was the best of which he was capable, after all, the performance of his life.

THE GIRL IN THE BLACK RAINCOAT

———————————————

You MIGHT FIND this all a little hard to believe, but try
looking at it like this: think of those bulletin board kind of
items you see in the back of the paper, the ones where the
people are looking for each other. *You brown jacket, blue
eyes/ me white scarf, red hair/ I smiled/ you got off 14th
st/ pls come to such and such a place at such and such a
time* . . . Like that. Like most reasonable people, probably,
I always thought these things were stupid, or maybe just
pathetic, the sad spectacle of all those people trying to get a
grip on the chips of straw that float along past them on the
downtown trains. But behind that I've also had a terrific
temptation to *do it*, not run an ad of my own, of course, but
sometime put on the scarf, the jacket, the eyes and smile
they asked for, turn myself into the person they wanted,
and show up. But that's not how it started.

I was going to meet Luisa at one of the new clubs they have — it had just opened up that week and I really didn't know anything about it. Luisa was one of these impossibly beautiful Latin women I used to see on the street fairly often and never at all expected to actually get to know. For one thing, there were always good arguments against it. In my neighborhood they tended to be very Catholic and to have lots and lots of relatives — all with a purely medieval vision of right relations between the sexes — including those clumps of the disaffected unemployed who stand around on the corners with nothing better to do all day than dream up ways to return some part of what's been handed to them back in the general direction of its source, maybe at the point of a knife or a gun or just along the sharp edge of some piece of something that might happen to be lying around nearby. Family honor is one of the few things some of these guys have left to protect, which encouraged me to look at the vivid beauties of my neighborhood as if they were flowers in the Brooklyn Botanic Gardens, a delight for the eye alone, or, better yet, for the short-term sidelong glance.

With Luisa this whole situation was turned around in kind of a funny way. She'd grown up in Queens, some- where around Middle Village. Her parents were dentists who operated a nice little mom-and-pop practice out of the ground floor of the place where they lived, with her mother doing the brushing and scraping and her father doing the more complicated dental science work. Luisa was born into this situation, and her English was better than her Spanish (that surprised me at first but it was true). She had one brother, who'd gone in the Navy to learn navigation and then become an officer in the merchant fleet. It was the American dream.

Meanwhile, owing to inertia, indecision, and a general lack of will, I was sinking backward into the American nightmare, not that I saw it that way myself. I'd landed on top of a wriggling chunk of San Juan slum transplanted to a section of the Brooklyn waterfront, a bit dirty and smelly and noisy but with cheap enough rent so I didn't have to work full time to make it, which was then my chief objective. Luisa hadn't grown up in any kind of place like that, but naturally she knew all about them, as I could see the first time I mentioned my address — a frown, a little silent whistle, and then a shining, masking smile.

I met her at work, which is computer programming. I was going to be something else but it didn't work out. But I was sitting there with all the skills I'd picked up incidentally, at a time when demand was comfortably ahead of supply, so it was an easy way to go. I work at such and such a place in midtown three days a week most weeks. There's quite a few programs that no one understands but me by this time, so I don't have to deal with people much. I'm just a kind of electronic mole down there, burrowing among all the machines, and that's okay with me. Anyway, I'd been a prog in this place for about six years when Luisa showed up as an op. Later on I discovered she was on the rebound from some atavistic episode of failed teenage rebellion which involved a very good-looking and stupid youngblood, some drugs, some bad risks, and possibly an abortion. Now she was turning it around with a keypunch job days, a couple of City College courses at night, and somewhere in between a nascent interest in older and seemingly brainy guys.

I tend not to notice anyone much down in the basement, a bright humming place full of the smell of electricity, where people can come to seem like a mistake. So Luisa might have been there as much as a week before I became completely aware of her. Likely I'd handed her a couple of things, maybe answered a couple of questions. Then one morning I was stuck on something and had swung away from the terminal trying to figure it, my head full of numbers and eyes tracking aimlessly along the concrete floor. All of a sudden here was this shoe, a plain black pump with a medium heel to it, and building out of the heel was a tendon standing tensely away from the bone with the intervening flesh pulled taut as a sail, rising to meet the flare of the calf muscle just under the cuff of a green-striped pair of pants . . . and on and on and on until I was looking at Luisa's bright mouth, with a plastic cup of coffee gliding toward it in the slim fingers of her hand. She winked at me and we both started laughing and that was the beginning of that.

Later, a little deeper into it all, you could see that she had a very clear idea of what she wanted and that I was not very likely to turn into that thing. I discovered she had the kind of bad temper I'd formerly associated strictly with redheads, which was exacerbated by the fact that I had one too, though it was buried fairly deep. So there you are, the seeds of failure, right there from the start, but I still say it was worth it.

Weekends, with the weather permitting, Luisa played on a women's soccer team over in East River Park. It was quite serious, with meets and matches and everything. I went a couple of times but it did something to me I didn't much like to see her go blazing at some other player like a runaway railroad train, so I quit going. She might have minded,

but she never said she did. So it was a Saturday and she had
got some passes for this club from somebody else on her
team or whatever. There was a game that day and the team
was going out to dinner after it, something I was planning
to skip, so the plan was for us to meet in Chelsea, in front of
the door of this club, which in and of itself was a mistake.

What I hadn't known about this place was that it was one
of the kind where there's velvet ropes outside on the sidewalk with some tinsel-brained goons standing behind them
to vet the clientele for looks and fashion sense and decide
who's good enough to come in. A *door policy* is what this
is called, and I had a private rule never to go to any place
with a door policy, which whatever it may have been worth
as a social statement stood to save me all kinds of incon-
venience and embarrassment, not to mention outbreaks of
blinding rage. So I wasn't too pleased to find myself breaking this rule of mine, standing on that stupid line just for a
chance to have this pair of flits in parody tuxedos pass some
kind of judgment on me. It being one of my absent-minded
days I hadn't really dressed for success either, just had on
old clothes and a worn-out windbreaker, and I wasn't even
warm enough, not really. Luisa wasn't there yet and I stood
around on the sidewalk for fifteen or twenty minutes, circling through the line, stepping aside to let people who'd
already made their connections get through and developing
a terminal dislike for this one guy on the door, an especially
nasty one with a snotty little flip of hair on his forehead
that just made me want to scalp him.

My mood was getting worse so fast that it already seemed
like too late to bail it out when Luisa finally did show up,
marching across the street with a couple of the other soccer
girls in tow and a sheaf of passes waving in her hand. She

was all in a flutter of haste herself, apparently late to meet someone else inside as well as me, so she didn't give me much of a hello, just slapped a pass in my hand and aimed me at the door. At this point things got a bit confusing — I think the soccer girls went in, and then the flit with the hair put his hands up like a traffic policeman, saying something I didn't quite catch, and pushed me back a little, pushed Luisa too. That cooked it. I just didn't have the proper humility to meet those particular circumstances, and the instant I felt that hand on my jacket my self-control checked out the window and my right hand went into my back hip pocket after this gargantuan pawn shop knife I had bought to keep me company at times when one of my programs caved in suddenly and I had to ride the trains through the lonelier parts of the night.

It wasn't much of a threat, this knife, being so dull it probably wouldn't have cut butter, but it was big and heavy enough to make a terrific paperweight and looked bad enough to have got me arrested or possibly shot. Luckily for all involved Luisa knew what was in that pocket and she got one hand locked on my wrist before I could get it out while with the other she reached around and gave me a sharp hard pinch on the back of the neck, which was enough to clear my head momentarily. I turned loose of the knife and we both pulled out of the crowd and walked off down the sidewalk into the dark, me leading the way.

I told her she should go on in and hook up with her friends, it was no big deal, I could catch up with her later, another night, and I actually did mean most of all that, but she wasn't having any. The fact was that I was so angry I felt like I was drunk, and I knew I wasn't going to be good company. Mostly I was mad at myself by that time, naturally. The first thing I wanted to do was get home and forget I ever left, and the last thing I wanted was to be around anyone who'd witnessed that latest piece of foolishness, but Luisa stuck to me, grim as death, even when I turned the corner and went stalking off down Seventh Avenue. The conversation had fizzled out by this time, and I couldn't hear anything but her heels going clip-clop on the pavement and my own pulse beating in my ears.

That got old fairly quickly, as you may imagine, and after a bit longer, just to break it up, I cut into a coffee shop, and we sat down in a booth by the window. I had a cup of coffee and she had a cup of tea and in a few minutes we started to talk, not about any of what had just happened but about the general outlines of the past and the future. It was a calm conversation, if kind of a sad one, and after about an hour we had got to the end of it, which seemed to be the end of us as well. Luisa was being very cool and reasonable about the whole thing, which was never the best of signs with her, but I was feeling so washed out and empty by the time we got done that I didn't really pick up the signal.

I paid our tab at the register and we went out the door and just as we got on the street Luisa turned back to me.

"You make me so mad you know, I'd like to hit you in the face." She said it in such a natural way that I assumed she was kidding.

"Go ahead, then," I said, and *zap* — something like a windmill blade sang past my head and I took a step back and my hands came up like they were loaded on springs. Long ago and far away I was in the Golden Gloves, no great white hope or anything like it, but I qualified and won three fights and took a TKO in the fourth from a black kid from Brownsville who almost made the Olympics later that year, I heard. That brought me back to my senses, somewhere around the age of sixteen, and no one had tried to hit me ever since. It was funny to see the reflexes were still there, and alarming to think of what they might do, but I still didn't understand Luisa was serious and I didn't believe it until when her next shot came hissing by I saw her purse go winding off her wrist and skid about halfway up the block.

Then I was thinking a lot of mixed-up things along a spectrum from *Hey, this is really happening* to *What am I doing with my hands here?* when I heard a single toot on a siren and a car thumped the curb with its front tires and out of it jumped a guy in a black leather jacket and no hat, who it took me a second to realize was a cop.

"You're not really doing this, are you?" he said. It was the perfect line and neither one of us was going to let it drop.

"No sir," I said. "You called it exactly right, we aren't doing a thing."

"We were just on our way home, that is," Luisa said, and she gave me a big stagy kiss on the cheek. I went and got her purse and gave it to her, and we wrapped our arms around each other and stood there like that until the police car was altogether out of sight. Then we looked at each other and we had to laugh and she gave me a real kiss and we had a sober handshake for goodbye, and that was how we ended friends in spite of everything. I don't know when I'd ever been so grateful for a cop.

.   .   .

Luisa went click-clack up the block to the subway, out of my love life, into the tired old designation of *ex*. I stood there and watched her out of sight and then I started walking downtown. The anger was all gone now but it had left me with that drained feeling a broken fever can leave. I went over to Broadway where everything was closed and kept on going south. In the dark plate-glass windows behind the gates I could see the outline of my reflection passing by in parallel with me, a phantasmal unknown quantity, just a shape with nothing clear inside of it. I kept walking faster, like I thought I was maybe going to pass it, but of course it cruised right along beside me the whole time.

The idea was that if I walked so fast I was half winded my head wouldn't be getting enough blood and oxygen to start going, and if I walked all the way home across the bridge I'd be so beat by the time I got there I could go right to sleep before any misgivings caught up with me. Then in the morning it would all be different. It was a trick I'd tried before and I remembered it had worked and since the club had been in Chelsea it looked like a plenty long enough walk to work this time too. Only I couldn't quite seem to get ahead of myself, though I went so fast I started a sweat which turned cold on me in the breeze of my own movement, and the rows of street lights up ahead began to go double and stream across my eyes.

No matter how hard you might try to do it, you can't take anything back. Oh, but I did wish I was not the person who had done some of the things I'd done that night. The business at the club was stupid and crazy enough to give most people a lot of discomfort, but that wasn't the worst of it for me. Somehow I just couldn't imagine that going any further, even though it easily could have. I couldn't see my-self actually cutting the kid with the hair or see the cops coming on the scene or see a muzzle flash that might have turned out to be the last thing I ever saw. What I *could* see was one of my hands, all by itself and without my ever planning it, hooking out into Luisa's face, tearing flesh and cracking bone, doing a thing neither of us could ever have forgiven me for. I kept seeing that over and over, plain as if it really had occurred, and every time it came around I wriggled and writhed like something had bitten me and I rushed to turn another corner as if doing that would put my thoughts on another track.

But all I could seem to do was open trap doors and hatches onto a lot of other things I'd have been happy enough not to recall. Most of the time it's easy enough to see yourself as being basically good. You'll look back over things you've done in your life and judge a fair number to be well inten-tioned and most of the rest of them harmless. There's the stuff that makes somebody it's not so hard to live with, but at other times, in other moods, you'll find you've committed acts enough to construct a completely different person, a regular evil bastard you could never bear to be. There's things you think you've wiped out or forgotten, left stran-gled in the tightening coil of your past, but nothing, more's the pity, is ever really lost. Comes a time when every shame-ful thing will rise up from the path before you and shriek its accusation and spit its bitter poison in your face. Other kinds of trouble can be avoided but in the end there's no outrunning the terror of what you might be and of what you are.

Well, all that's only a mood, of course, and there's other

moods that can replace it. But in this case my system wasn't working. I kept running and rerunning everything I'd ever wished I'd never done, all the way back to small cruelties to my little brother and maybe wicked thoughts I'd had in the cradle too. After a while I couldn't stand it anymore. I'm not quite sure where I was exactly but it was somewhere in Little Italy. I'd been walking quite a while and it was really late by this time, but here came a window lit with neon beer signs, and I pulled the door beside it open and went in.

If you're sitting at a bar the first thing you're apt to notice is a mirror and naturally I did my best to ignore that part of the scene. I caught the eye of the bartender, a guy with a lumpy bald head and a cigar stuck in his mouth like it grew there. He drew me a beer and I drank it. A trick I learned in college and hadn't had much use for since: you just open up your gullet and pour it down like it was flat and you were dumping it down the sink. I had another one the same way and then I waited. In a minute there came a peeling ripping sensation like what I imagine a snake might feel when it finally comes out of its dirty used-up skin. I looked at myself in the mirror then and it was just another stranger. Safe and home free at last. I swung around with my back to the bar and looked to see what kind of place I was in.

Dark woodwork climbing the walls, three square tables set at angles on black and white checkerboard tile, juke box, an enclosed phone booth, and another pay phone on the wall. At one of the tables there was a young couple talking quietly. The rear wall was painted green and there was a triple-width arch that let into a room in the back. More tables were in the back room, laid with white cloths, with no one sitting at them. The juke box wasn't playing and it was so quiet I could hear the buzz of the ice chests rise and fall.

A big brindled cat came walking out of the back and hopped onto the bar and then down on the other side. When the cat was gone I was still looking at the space behind it and there was a big painting covering the whole wall there, so big the figures were almost life size: a café or trattoria that might have been in Greece or Italy, some Mediterranean country where clean white sunlight fell through a latticed ceiling on the white-aproned owner standing solid in the middle of the picture and on all his customers at the tables behind. It was queer how familiar it seemed, like something you've half remembered from a dream, and then I glanced at the bartender and he and the man in the picture were the same, right down to the length of that chewed cigar. An odd feeling that gave me, coming hard after the breathless walk and the beer, like the picture tore a little hole between one world and another and the two worlds were sucking at each other through the gap.

The bartender read my look his own way and brought me another beer which I poured into me the same way I had the others. As I was setting the bottle back down a little motion behind me made me turn. The guy at the table had reached across to the girl and caught her hand just as she was striking a match to a cigarette. I was wondering why, why he would do that, and then I saw she already had a fresh one going in the ashtray at her elbow.

It was like I had accidentally looked at something private, and I turned partly away, but I kept on looking at them out of the corner of my eye. I felt very calm now and it was almost like TV. The girl hitched her chair a little away from the table and that way I could see her better. She was all swaddled up in a black raincoat, big on her and buttoned all the way down to the ankles, so the only other thing you could see she had on was her shoes. Her arm, a thin white arm, came out of the black sleeve and took up the cigarette and drew it back toward her face. I sat there and watched her watch it burn. At first I wouldn't have said she was good looking. For instance, she was nothing like Luisa, no clear definition of feature, but kind of a shapeless face, all smooth inside the ring of her deep black hair. But then one expression came over her face and then another, the looks succeeding and changing into each other the way the surface of a lake is changed by movement in the sky. Then the changes stopped and she took a long pull at the cigarette and set it back on the lip of the ashtray where it had been before and after a moment let a long white column of smoke float out of her toward the ceiling.

The guy was looking at her the whole time too. There wasn't such a mystery about the way he looked; I'd call it just plain miserable. Again I had that twinge of déjà vu, a sense I'd watched the scene before from a different angle. The girl stood up and knocked on the table and came walking very slowly toward the bar. Yes, she was very pretty now.

She rested lightly against the curl of wood at the edge of the bar, one foot raised on the rail. Her hair hung forward, so that all I could see of her profile was the tip of her nose. She raised two fingers to the bartender, who came over with a bottle of beer and a shot glass he filled with vodka for her. When she tossed her head back to drink the shot I saw the curve of her mouth and her cheek. After she put the glass back on the bar she reached somewhere inside the raincoat and came out with a cigarette and a yellow book of matches. I was that close to reaching over and stopping her; it seemed like such a natural thing to do, but I caught myself in time. She lit the cigarette, blew smoke, turned and looked me full in the face. I thought, *Oh no, I can't use it now*, but I couldn't break the glance, not right away. Then she had turned back toward her table and I was out the door and walking to the subway.

Home was the only thing on my mind. I was dead tired all through my body down to the blisters on my feet. The platform was empty and quiet as the grave. I had been waiting ten minutes, pacing from pole to pole, when a man and a dog came down the steps. The man laid out a double-width sleeping bag he'd been carrying rolled under one arm. He and the dog both got into it and lay there back to back.

The mouth of the tunnel had had a hollow unused feel before, but it was the man and the dog going to bed on the platform that convinced me there'd really be a long wait for the train. I took a seat and hunched into it, letting my eyes fall shut. Somewhere near her stop in Queens, Luisa was getting her purse snatched, then leading a band of other fed-up citizens to run down the thief and recover it. I was falling into a sleep so sound I would miss all the trains and not wake up till morning, stiff and cold, panicky at first, then relieved that the night had passed without any terrible harm being done, then just grateful that, after all, I was still alive.

Luisa would make the morning paper, and on Monday at work she'd have a season of celebrity, and I'd congratulate her on her luck and boldness no more nor less whole-heartedly than the others. That still belonged to what I didn't know yet, but I did know we had lost each other; we were just another chance encounter now, drifting on the stream of time. How much easier it always is to lose something than to have anything to lose! But I let that thought go and slept remembering the girl in the black raincoat, how she had looked at me just as if we'd known each other for all of a thousand years. Hard to believe, impossible to verify, but it was there, that flash of contact, like a match scraping into a blue flame that showed us briefly each to the other, two separate dreamers of the dream of love.

I'VE GOT
A SECRET

WHAT WERE YOU, SLEEPING? My God, I thought
you never would answer the phone. One of these days, Sid,
you're going to just nod out and never come back, that's
what. You can just remember I said so. I never knew anyone, my whole life long, who could just sit there like that
and look at a ringing telephone and not reach over and pick
it up. Even if you don't feel like talking you'd think you'd
at least be a little curious. What you could be missing, you
know? It could be something extra special, good news,
something wonderful. It even could be little Crystal calling. *Me*.

No, it's unnatural for a person not to answer the phone.
It just isn't normal, I can hardly imagine it even, what it
would feel like to do such a thing. Unplug it, switch the
machine on maybe, but just sit there and listen to it, no way.
I mean, even if you *are* doing a lot of scag, that's really kind

of special. I mean, it's beyond low motivation, really out there, you know, that's something I'd never understand if I knew you for a thousand years.

But while we're on the subject, I'm pretty sure I've got a line on some China White. That's right, the old original death trip itself, one cut was what I heard, though of course I don't believe *that*. And in fact I might be able to get a little taste of it for maybe a special friend, and such a good *listener*, too. It's just barely possible I could do that . . . Because I do need someone to talk to today. Just talk and talk and talk and talk and talk and talk and *talk*. I'm in that kind of mood, you know? And no, you don't have to answer. Don't worry, you don't have to say a single word.

Now. Have I got your attention?

You know, have you ever had one of those days when you wake up and you don't like your skin? I mean, you just don't *like* it. When your whole surface just seems so unattractive, sort of. I must have spent I don't know how long in the shower, till all the hot water was out anyway, not that that takes so long in this miserable skinflint cheapo building, it must have a boiler the size of a coffee pot at least. Well I stood in the shower forever it seemed like and I still just *didn't like my skin.* There's nothing wrong with it, I don't have a rash or anything, just a little tear around my cuticle, and I peeled that off. And that made me wonder, What if I could just go on peeling and tearing and peeling and tearing? Like a snake rubbing up on a rock, just rubbing that old skin right off, till pretty soon out comes the whole shiny new-looking snake.

Well naturally I know a person couldn't actually *do* that. I mean if you did there wouldn't be anything under there but a bunch of bloody muscles, right? Like those see-through pictures they used to have in the science books, the old kind with the sex parts left out. That's all there is up under there is a lot of stringy old raw meat. Well anyway the hot water ran out and I still feel like I have soap on me or something, though the fact is I spent at least a half hour rinsing it off. So then I was just thinking about who could I call? Then I thought maybe old Sid might be interested in what the guy said — it wasn't Howie either so you don't have to hang up and call him — about how he was going to step on the stuff one or two more times and then try to sell it in speedballs maybe. At parties and clubs and things like that. What a waste, huh, Sidney? But he just doesn't seem like the type to go for the rough trade. Then again, *we* probably know quite a few people who would go for a speedball occasionally. We might be able to work something out on a commission basis, don't you think?

But before I do anything I've got to start feeling better. I've just got to get in a better mood somehow. I need to start liking my skin again, and things. Because right now I feel like I'm stuck in one of those greasy-soap-film commercials. Only I know it's just a mental thing. Dial or whatever would never take it off, supposing there was even any hot water, that is. I guess I'll just have to talk it out. That's if you don't mind, of course. And you *don't* mind, do you, Sid?

You know, if you could just get yourself to say a few things *back*, like "How do you *feel* about that?" and "Tell me more," you probably could actually make money just listening to people over the phone. Only you couldn't start charging me. Not little Crystal. That would have to be our deal, okay?

Anyhow, I did think I might see you at the party last

night. After I put *two* messages on your machine about it. I guess you didn't bother playing it back, maybe? That's what I'd call *apathetic*. No, I'm not fishing for an apology. After all, it's no one's loss but your own if you missed it. Missed meeting that interesting guy with the China White, too.

Still, I'd have thought you'd want to see what Sheldon's new loft was like, all fixed up and everything. Even if Sheldon himself is a bit on the tedious side. But what he has done with that *place*. And the *money* he must have spent. You could practically see yourself in the floor. Then there's that perfectly gorgeous view, two walls of windows, and he's even got a little garden or whatever fixed on the roof, though of course it was too cold to stay up there very long. Still, it made a good place to slip away to for a moment of privacy, if you know what I mean.

It was a classy party, too. I mean they even had *steak tartare*. Which I love with a perfect passion, not that you'd understand. I just can't comprehend how a human being could be as indifferent to food as you are. But this was just right, with lots of lemon, and capers, and anchovies, and hunks of French bread to eat it on. I could have eaten up half the dish, I swear. Only they say now it can make you sick, something to do with what they feed the poor cows, I don't know. I do wish I'd never ever heard about that, it made it practically turn to stone in my mouth when I thought of it, that wonderful steak tartare. Everything's poison now, isn't that a shame? But I thought, *All right, I'll just drink, then*. There must have been a truckload of champagne.

The only problem was I really didn't know anybody all that well, you know? I mean Sheldon was busy flitting about, of course. It really would have been helpful if you'd showed up. It looks so awkward if you're not talking to someone at a party. You feel like people are just watching you eat and drink. And there was this wormy little guy who started staring at me over by the food table, before I'd remembered that thing about raw beef. Really a nasty-looking little person. He was part bald and he'd shaved the rest, I always hate the way that looks. Like a thing out from under a rock. Well I didn't know if I'd gone mental or what but it seemed like he was watching me wherever I moved to after that. He didn't really seem to be talking to anybody himself, and he didn't even have a drink. And it wasn't like he was trying to catch my eye, either. No, it seemed like he was looking at my mouth, right at my *mouth*, the whole time, I mean, it made me very self-conscious. Did you ever hear of anything so queer?

So that's why I was so pleased when I saw Marlan come in. Someone I know, for God's sake, even if we had had a little spat. She was with Weber and Jimmy Sinclair and that mousy little Gwen and a few other people, a whole gaggle in fact. Well by that time I was so freaked out with that little toad staring at my mouth all the time that I practically fell on her neck.

And that was a mistake, Sid, it really was a mistake. It was like I flung myself at her and missed and hit the wall. I'm speaking figuratively now, of course. But I mean, that was what it felt like. Oh, she said hello and everything. But there I was, practically ready to kiss her, and her whole affect was like *Oh. Oh yes. Oh I do know you, don't I.* That kind of thing. Well of course we both knew it was an act. Still, it was embarrassing for me, people were watching.

I don't see why she needs to be so snooty, I mean we've

known each other five or six years now, a lot of water under the bridge there, you know. Even if we were never really all that close, but I do think Marian has that fear of intimacy or whatever they call it, at least she does with me. Anyhow, I never would have expected her to hang onto a grudge like that. I mean so what if I made a little pass at her precious boyfriend, it was six months ago for God's sake. And it isn't as if anything came of it at *all*. Not as if it was successful. I mean anyone would know it was just a party kind of thing, a few drinks and a little propinquity, Christ, I don't even really *like* Weber if it comes to that. It could have happened to anybody. And the winner's supposed to be magnanimous or something, isn't that right?

Not Marian though, no way. Really, ever since she took up with Weber almost she's been so sort of *serious*, in not a very nice way at all. When she used to be so much *fun*. I can remember Marian with a speedball in her, she could be absolutely devastating. So easy to be with too, but all that's a long time gone. She and Weber, it's like they bring out this moral attitude in each other, and I wouldn't call it pleasant, not really. Maybe most of it comes from him in the first place, but they're so goddamned self-righteous, both of them, really.

Well I hardly felt like talking to anybody else in that little group, not after Marian came on so nasty. So I just sailed away and got myself another glass of champagne. It was Freixenet, well, that's not Moët of course, but good enough. A little later I tried to chat with Gwen but she really doesn't have much spark. I've never had a lot to say to Jimmy anyway, and of course Weber wasn't going to make any conversation. It would have been difficult for both of us really, after Marian had been so hateful.

So I just kicked back and watched them all. And you know, after I pulled myself together, I started to get the feeling that something was up with him and her. Everything wasn't quite so rosy-cosy, the way it used to be. There was just a little vibration, a fault line you might call it, something I could kind of sense, though it wasn't anything real specific. Just a kind of tension. They split up practically the minute they came in the room. Weber went over with Jimmy and some other guys and stood around where the liquor was, of course. Marian was cruising. It seemed like she knew everybody there. She just kept going around in a circle. It was just regular party behavior, you know, but there was something off, something I couldn't quite get at first. I noticed she was drinking vodka, just over ice, straight to the hard stuff, that's Marian for you, and it seemed like every five minutes she was fixing another glass.

That's when I finally did catch on, it was always *another* glass, never the same one. She'd set down her drink to light a cigarette or shake hands or whatever and never pick it up. Then a minute later she'd be pouring herself another one. Once you noticed it was really quite peculiar. And then I saw she was doing the exact same thing with cigarettes. A drag or two, then down in an ashtray, and she'd never find it again, just light up the next one. Well, that can get to be an expensive kind of carelessness after a while, I mean the drinks were free. If she had started bumming from me, for instance, it would have been hard to be sympathetic.

But really, it was very weird. I looked over at Weber finally and I saw he saw it too. It was like he positively flinched that somebody else had noticed. And maybe that was what gave me the idea of how I could get to Marian a little. She'd been so nasty to me, and I thought, Why not make her feel a little creepy? All I had to do was watch her. Watch her and follow her around the room from a few yards away, like that wormy little runt had been doing me. He was still doing it, too. It was all a little bit nutty, I guess. All it would have taken was for Marian to get interested in watching *him* and we would have had some kind of sicko version of *A Midsummer Night's Dream*. Anyhow, it *did* work. I could tell it was getting to her, and the best thing was, I realized, that she couldn't be sure I was doing anything on purpose. But I knew it was really bugging her because after a while she went off and tried to hide in the kitchen.

Now the kitchen was one thing about Sheldon's place that wasn't quite what it should have been. I mean there was all sorts of wonderful kitchen stuff in there, but the thing was it was totally enclosed instead of being open to the rest of the space, just a little white box there really. It was sort of claustrophobic actually, which was why nobody had grouped up in there, because it was a pretty big party. Marian went straight to the freezer of course, and what did she find there but a bottle of vodka, the good Russian kind, I guess Sheldon hadn't wanted to put it out. I was just standing there by the doorway thinking, when she looked up that would finish her off. But she didn't notice me right away.

She set the bottle down on the counter and started turning around and around in the kitchen. I guessed she was looking for a glass at first but she didn't open a cabinet or anything like that, just kept turning and turning like a dog trying to make up its mind where to lie down. Then all of a sudden she stopped in front of the sink and reached out and turned on the cold water. She stuck both her wrists under the tap and just held them there like that, like she was trying to bring down a fever or something. It made me cold just to look at it. She stayed that way for a long time, just standing there with her eyes shut and that cold, cold water running down over her arms.

Oh, Sid, I just can't tell you how that made me feel. It's silly but I felt like I wasn't mad anymore at all. I was just swollen up with some kind of feeling I couldn't really have named exactly. It was like Marian was in some terrible kind of trouble and all I wanted to do, for a minute anyway, was try to lead her out of it. It was like I just wanted to hold her and rock her to sleep. It was the strangest thing.

"Marian," I said, and that was a mistake too, because I hadn't quite worked out what I wanted to say yet. Maybe I was just a little bit tiddly by this time. She looked up with the most peculiar expression, like she had such an awful headache she could just barely peep around it to see what was going on outside her own head. It seemed like she really didn't recognize me this time, like it wasn't an act at all anymore. Well, that did get me a little annoyed.

"Are you not feeling *well*, dear?" I said to her. "You must have lit twenty cigarettes and poured twenty drinks the last half hour, what is *with* you, anyway?"

Well I shouldn't have said that either, of course. That headachy expression disappeared in a flash and the way she looked at me I thought I was some kind of bug or germ looking up through the wrong end of the microscope at some enormous eye.

"Well, what is it?" I said. Because obviously she was about to make some kind of remark.

"No," she said. "I'm not going to say it." And she tried to get by me, out of the kitchen.

"Oh, come on now," I said. "Now you've got my curiosity up. Penny for your thoughts."

So then she kind of bit her lip.

"All right, Crystal," she said. "Since you insist. I was just thinking that you are the most tiresome nosy meddling little bitch I have ever had the misfortune to be personally acquainted with. And now would you *please* get out of my way."

Which you can imagine I was happy to do by that time. Oh yes, I couldn't let her out of there soon enough. Off she stalked, and I just stood there unable to move practically, I felt like I'd been run over by a train. Imagine the nerve of her! But she really does know how to tear a person down. Well I thought I'd never speak to her again, of course, but just then it was hard to imagine she'd care very much.

I think I'm a little bit clairvoyant, Sid, I know you don't believe it but I'm sure I've got just a touch of ESP or something. I was propped up on the wall of that little bitty kitchen, trying to cope with the shock somehow, when I got this certain feeling that I knew was going to be true. I just knew that Marian would be talking to me again someday. Oh, not that she was ever going to say she was sorry, not her. But one day before too long we were going to be as good friends again as we ever were. Because she was going to need somebody. *Anybody*. She was going to need me, and I could feel it in my bones. So that made me feel a little better.

Then when I looked up there was that same wormy little guy standing in the doorway like some kind of a horrible copycat. It was really getting to be time to do something about that. So I just marched right over to him.

"Well, *hi* there," I said. Bright as you please. It was enough to frighten the life out of him of course. "You've been following me around all night," I said. "And I was beginning to wonder just what in the hell you want."

He hemmed and hawed for an hour, it seemed like. And the queer thing was even now we were talking face to face he still wouldn't look me in the eye. He just kept right on staring into my mouth, like he wanted to see what my tonsils looked like, or something. No shame, really, not the least bit.

"I just thought you might like a little toot" was what he finally managed to choke out. And really, it didn't sound like such a bad idea by that time. I really did kind of *need* it. And it was getting pretty late and the way things had been going I was beginning to doubt if anything much better was going to come along. And in the end he didn't turn out to be *so* bad really, though I wouldn't say I hadn't had better. But the kind of night I'd been having, I didn't really want to be alone. I wouldn't even *think* of seeing him again though, not if I hadn't thought *you* might be interested. Only in a business way, of course.

But before we left we went up on the roof. He didn't even tell me what it really was at first, which was kind of a crazy way to go about it. Naturally I was assuming it was coke. I mean, what if I hadn't had any experience, I might have gotten really sick. I don't know what he could have been thinking. As it was, even I felt pretty terrible for a minute. It's pretty straight stuff, Sid, though one cut would be saying a little too much. For a few seconds I had this awful feeling I was going to have to flop across the guard rail and just barf my heart out all over West Broadway. You know how it is when you misjudge your dose. But after a minute or so I felt all right again. I felt absolutely marvelous, in fact. It was more than just the rush, too. I felt like I had been right up to the edge of something dreadful and just barely pulled back in time. Like I'd just barely pulled back from something really bad. Have you ever had that feeling, Sid? Do you know what I'm talking about? *Do* you? *Are you listening to me?*

THE
KICK

<hr>

IN THE MIDDLE of the second brown belt form Sinclair
knew that Weber had beaten him again. Sinclair was halfway through the long high-tension move that always slowed
him down, dragging his fists up toward his forehead, his
forward foot grooving the floor as he pulled it back, when
he heard Weber break and go into the double jab. He'd lost
a half second and would never make it back, not honestly,
not with his uniform snapping on every block and punch.
Still, he tore through the rest of the form as fast as he could,
and when he heard Weber split the air with a deafening
kyai, slamming himself into the last double knife hand block,
Sinclair was almost into his own. *Bang bang*, he could hear
his heart, and he held his position, low in the back stance,
watching a bead of sweat roll down the hollow of his ex-
tended left wrist. Behind him the stranger was still not
finished with the form and Sinclair could hear his short

sharp breaths. *He's slow*, he thought, *a slow one*. Though his own arms and shoulders were trembling a bit, he wasn't tired, not really.

There came the pop of the last block and the visitor's *kyai* followed it, long and sustained. Weber shouted a Korean word and he and Sinclair came to attention in unison, bowing after a short pause, though no one was before them. Brown belt was the highest rank in this club, and Weber ran the class. Sinclair let his body relax so thoroughly that even his eyes went out of focus, using the slack time for every ounce it was worth. Then Weber, a blur, came walking around in front of him and he pulled himself together. Although Weber's hair was plastered to his head with sweat and something pulsed hard under his sternum, he seemed perfectly composed. With his left hand he motioned for the visitor to step out, and Weber and Sinclair bowed to each other. They had a standing bet that whoever came in behind in the second form would repeat it to the other's command. Sinclair outweighed Weber by a lot and outreached him by a little, and he could make it all pay in sparring, but Weber was very hard to beat on speed. Sinclair watched him drawing in his breath.

"ssshhhmmmMMEEEAAARRGGGHH!!!!!"

With all his muscles tight and vibrating, Sinclair drew his feet together and pulled his right fist into the cup of his left palm. He stood, feet touching, eyes focused on an imaginary point in the air a couple of yards ahead, where a leap and a twist would carry him.

"*Begin!*"

Sinclair threw himself into the first block and whipped around to the second pair. *Speed and power, don't give up one to the other*. His thoughts stopped there and buried themselves in his body. They did not turn back into words again until he reached that same troublesome high-tension move and thought he might be going to faint. Then Weber stepped in and gave him a target for the jab, and Sinclair's consciousness shut off. Weber stayed just ahead of him through the rest of the form, with Sinclair following him, snapping each technique almost against the white cotton of Weber's uniform. He was not Sinclair anymore anyway, only raw will in controlled and abstracted motion. At the moment of the last block and scream he felt his heart fly out of his mouth and hover in midair for an instant before it returned.

"*K'mon*," Weber said. "*Sho.*"

Sinclair came to attention, bowed, and relaxed. For a split second he felt absolutely terrific and then his stomach began to clutch, pumping hard on nothing like a strong empty hand. It felt like a heart attack was going on in his stomach. Pride prevented him from falling on the floor in a fit of the dry heaves.

"Endorphins not kicking in on schedule?" Weber smiled.

"Oh, go to hell," Sinclair said.

"Rest," Weber said, his face draining of expression, and then to the visitor, "Black belt forms?"

The visitor, who'd been kneeling to one side, got up and came forward. Sinclair walked to a corner and began to stretch, watching him. His nausea had subsided and every strand of his body glowed in its own deep heat. Sunk in a side split, he began to do arm rolls so as not to get stiff before sparring.

The visitor bowed to Weber, who began to count him

through the first black belt form. Sinclair saw that he still moved slowly, though he was always crisp, completing the hand techniques well after his feet were set. His belt and uniform were two different shades of black; the uniform washed to a paler, purplish shade. Sinclair did neck rolls; he could feel his shoulders getting cold. He was uneasy about the visitor, who looked like a biker type to him. The black uniform was not a good sign either. He'd proposed the notion to Weber, who had not agreed. So far the biker, if he was a biker, had observed all the complicated courtesies involved in visiting a strange school.

Sinclair put the soles of his feet together and watched the black belt go through the first form without count. He was still slow. His stances were good, but almost exaggeratedly low, and Sinclair thought that might be slowing him down. Behind him the lower belts, about fifteen of them ranging from yellow to purple, sat cross-legged, watching attentively but without perceptible expression. They were all young, all students at the high school, and all Hispanic except for three or four blacks. They were all small too; it was usually the small ones who took up karate, anywhere. Sinclair had always just had a complete lack of physical self-confidence in spite of the fact that he was really a little above average size. Weber was tall too, but he'd always been a rail, an elongated prototype of the ninety-seven-pound weakling.

The black belt was finishing the second form without count. Sinclair watched him work through the claw hands, another slow sustained-tension move. He looked good enough on stuff that was supposed to be slow, anyway. But he didn't pick up the pace any on the rest of the form and Sinclair let his eyes wander off around the little gym.

They practiced on a basketball court at off hours — at least it was a wooden floor. The collapsible bleachers at either end had been folded back to make a little more room for basics. A couple of bent hoops were cantilevered from the ceiling. The black belt hit the last position of the second form and held it, waiting for the command. Sinclair glanced over at him and saw, where his uniform had parted, the beginnings of a tattoo on the underside of his left pectoral. It was the sort of amateur tattoo that is done with a knife point and India ink and Sinclair couldn't see enough of it to tell what it was supposed to represent, but he didn't like the look of it at all.

Weber called the black belt to attention and they bowed to one another and relaxed. Sinclair got up, shaking out his legs as Weber clapped his hands.

"Line up for sparring," Weber called. The lower belts all got up quickly and came toward him, and Weber arranged them by gesture in two lines facing each other. Sinclair saw him pair the black belt with a purple belt and he came up and drew Weber away out of earshot.

"Do you really think you ought to let him fight?"

Weber drew his thumb along the edge of his lower lip. His eyes were sunken and serious under the heavy mat of black hair.

"You think not?"

"Well, look at him . . ." Sinclair took hold of Weber's sleeve and turned him back toward the lines. The fighters stood loosely with their hands open at their sides and their feet together, waiting. The visitor and the purple belt, a sweet-natured black boy of seventeen named Carleton, were at the head.

"He's kind of a big son of a bitch, don't you think?" Sinclair said. The black belt was at least as tall as Sinclair and must have outweighed him by twenty pounds, all meat. "I still think he's a biker or something like that."

"He's awfully clean for one," Weber said. "Look at all that clean hair."

It was true that the black belt had a wonderfully cared-for head of strawberry-blond hair. The hair was perfectly straight and had been pulled back in a thick rope through what looked like a napkin ring, hanging in the center of his back. His high cheekbones and the lines of the hair, which had been parted in the middle, gave him the aspect of a TV Indian.

"Did you happen to see that tattoo?" Sinclair said.

"Hm," Weber said. "Your average biker wouldn't come here alone, though. They like to travel in pairs, at least. Also, he's been very polite all along, you notice."

"He's slow, too," Sinclair said, more for his own comfort than anything else. It suddenly occurred to him that people with that kind of sluggishness came out of full-contact schools as often as not. But it was Weber's class and his decision. Sinclair just came up for Friday practice.

"It's not a tournament, after all," Weber said. "I'll tell them to go easy. We could sit out ourselves and watch them if you want."

"Good," Sinclair said. "I think that would be a very good idea."

"Okay," Weber said, raising his voice for the others, walking back toward them. "Instructional sparring. No contact. Be careful. No contact."

The two lines rippled. Weber and Sinclair stood at the head, looking down the space between them.

"Bow," Weber said, and paused. "Begin."

The lines spread out and scattered into pairs, the fighters circling each other. The convention of instructional sparring was for lower belts to attack and upper belts to counter. The upper belts had the right to stop the bout to offer advice whenever they felt it was called for. Sinclair watched Carleton explore the black belt with two side kicks off the front leg. Nothing special. The black belt backed off the first and blocked the second. He did not counter, although Sinclair thought the block had opened up some possibilities.

"Let's move back a little," Weber said. He and Sinclair went to stand against a corner of the bleachers. Carleton, intent, very serious, edged in and threw a knife hand from way too far out and then a roundhouse kick that had a better chance. The black belt stopped it with an X block.

"Ouch," Sinclair said. The block had connected high on the ankle where he knew it would bruise.

"There's a little lesson there, though, isn't there," Weber said.

"Sure," Sinclair said absently.

Carleton was approaching again, more tentative now. Sinclair saw the black belt skip forward and lash out with a hook kick off his front leg, leading with the heel. "Lord, he's not so slow after all," Sinclair said out loud. Carleton ducked it on reflex and bobbed back up and Sinclair saw the kick reverse itself without sinking an inch and then the black belt's instep slammed into the side of Carleton's head. The boy went down limp and Sinclair and Weber ran for him. Weber got there first and turned him on his back, feeling around the temple area with flexed fingers. Sinclair knelt beside him in time to see Carleton's eyes flutter open.

"How many fingers?" Weber was saying, and Carleton got it right, three, and then Sinclair and Weber helped him to the bleachers. Sinclair pulled out the bottom rack so he would have a place to sit.

"I'm okay," Carleton said. He smiled, shook his head, and winced. "Okay, I think, just let me rest a little. I'll sit one out." He leaned back and closed his eyes and Weber beckoned Sinclair to the corner.

"What do you think?" Sinclair said softly.

"I think he's probably all right. I can't feel anything too major. It was a slap kick."

"The bastard has nice extension, doesn't he? If he'd hit him with the ball we'd have a dead purple belt on our hands."

"I know. I'll have to get him to a doctor anyway. Check for hairlines and explain about concussion and all that wonderful stuff. Rafael can take him, they're buddies." Weber shrugged. "I thought I heard you say he was slow."

"Was that all you heard me say? Well, now I say he's a hustler. Or do you think that was an accident?"

"I don't care, tell you the truth. It'll be the last one he has around here, that's all."

Weber shouted for Rafael, who broke out of the group and jogged over, a stocky Puerto Rican boy with very white, even teeth, a green belt. Sinclair looked over at the others. The sparring had stopped of its own accord and all the lower belts stood in a half circle around the black belt, who was kneeling on the floor, sitting back on his heels, hands spread open on his knees. That was the correct posture to assume after a sparring accident, but Sinclair did not believe in the least it had really been an accident. The lower belts were quiet and probably none of them had really seen it clearly, but all their loyalty would be with their own. They were just waiting for Weber to tell them what to do.

Sinclair did not think that the black belt could possibly be crazy enough to take on the whole school. At the worst they would just have to form a line and walk him out of the building.

Rafael was helping Carleton toward the door, with one of Carleton's arms pulled over his own shoulders, and Sinclair saw Weber start back toward the center of the court. There was something wrong about the jerky way he was walking but Sinclair didn't catch on quite in time. Weber stopped, cocked his left arm, and slapped it with the heel of his right hand. The crack of the contact was shockingly loud. Then Sinclair saw the black belt get up with a flicker of a smile crossing his face and thought, *Oh no, this is his way, don't play it his way you idiot . . .* With a sick lowering in his stomach he saw it was impossible for him to protest or interfere in front of Weber's lower belts, too late for anything like that now.

The black belt and Weber exchanged the distrust bow, not breaking eye contact, and fell back into fighting stances. For a second neither moved. Sinclair stepped in closer. He would much rather have been in Weber's place himself; that way at least the weight and range would be closer to even. Weber looked almost frail, lost in his uniform. It was unbelievably stupid for him to have let himself be maneuvered into a man-by-man elimination. Sinclair rocked on the balls of his feet. If Weber went down he would be in charge and he had just decided that he would order everyone to jump on the black belt and tear him to pieces then, but he wanted to get in first himself if possible.

The black belt came in and Weber backed up at an angle. The black belt turned and came in again and Weber cut the other way. The lower belts had to scatter to make room for him. The black belt kept sidling forward and Weber stopped. He stood in a short cat stance with all his weight committed to his back leg. The stance declared certain overt weaknesses, but it was an invitation which Sinclair knew from experience could be risky to accept.

The black belt hopped in, leading with that same hook kick, and Sinclair was thinking *I wouldn't try that twice in a row* when Weber hit the floor. For a heart-stopping second Sinclair thought he was hit and then saw the side kick shooting up with the whole floor to brace against. Weber's heel and the curved edge of his foot drove in deep just above and to the left of the knot in the other's belt, lifting him a good six inches off the floor. Sinclair saw the black belt's feet go limp and dangle and knew that it was definitely over.

Weber didn't know, or didn't care. He followed the black belt through a roll onto his back and planted a twist punch middle target, hitting full power to the solar plexus. The black belt's mouth opened in a little moue, though there was no more air in there to be beaten out, Sinclair could see. He snatched Weber by the collar.

"You got him," he said. "You got him already, stop." Weber's left hand was cocked at his hip. "Lay off or you're going to kill him."

Weber shook his head, the motion of a dog worrying something. Then Sinclair felt his arm and shoulder loosen. Sinclair reached around him to examine the black belt, whose eyes, slack in the lids, were showing lines of white. Brushing the back of his hand under the black belt's nostrils, he got the feel of breath and the pulse was all right too when he found it in the wrist. Then the black belt's arm stiffened and pulled away.

Sinclair stood up and backed off a little, to stand beside Weber. The black belt sat forward, hands crossed over his stomach. Then he got all the way up. His hands rose to chest level and he looked like he might say something. Weber shifted his feet, pointing his left hip forward. The black belt took a deep breath and flinched. He pressed his hands against his side, one on top of the other.

"That's it," Sinclair said. "Just go on home." The black belt said nothing. He was looking down at the floor.

"Go on, now," Sinclair said. He felt like he was talking to a horse or something else that didn't understand anything but tone. Without saying anything the black belt turned and walked toward the door, where he had left his bundled street clothes. Sinclair followed him at a comfortable distance. The black belt picked up his roll and tucked it against his side and went out the door without looking back.

Weber had formed the class into ranks and was addressing them. He spoke very quietly but Sinclair could hear him perfectly well from where he stood by the door.

"People are always going to outweigh you and outreach you," Weber was saying. "They can be faster and better and sometimes they will be. There's not a whole lot you can do about that."

He paused. *Always the one for the little moral lessons*, Sinclair thought.

"But you don't ever have to let them outsmart you," Weber said. "Keep that in mind all the time." He turned shortly and walked toward Sinclair across the basketball court markings on the floor. The class stood, facing forward, where he had left them.

"Are you a freaking hero now?" Sinclair said. "Is that what's happening?"

"Not particularly," Weber said, veering off to the right. "Could you take finishing basics for me? I need to hit some wood."

Sinclair looked after him as he walked to the bleachers. Then Sinclair went to the head of the class. Each face was masked, trying hard to show nothing, but Sinclair, looking at them all, could begin to imagine how Weber might have felt it necessary to do the stupid thing he had done. All very well for him to talk about brain work, but he'd staked too much on that fancy fall, in Sinclair's opinion, and if it hadn't worked there'd have been no return. There was a thundering crash from behind him and Sinclair knew without having to look that Weber had just hit the bleachers with a side kick. The bleachers were rattling back against the wall with all their springs ringing softly. Weber was capable of keeping this up for a long time and certainly he would keep it up for the duration of finishing basics. Sinclair decided he would give everybody a good one.

"All right," he said. "Front kicks. Left leg first. With *kyai*. One. Two. Three . . ."

Weber and Sinclair came out of the showers last and walked down a narrow hall lined with lockers that had once been blue. Most of the paint had been hammered off them and now they were dented and torn and written all over with Magic Marker drawings and slogans. The hallway had a bad feel to it, partly because the ceiling was low, and Sinclair felt as if the lockers were always hedging in from both sides. Weber had a joke, if it was a joke, that he had started the karate class here just so he would feel he had some support somewhere when he had to walk down corridors like this one.

Weber had always claimed that he loathed his job at the school, which was teaching English. It turned out to be remedial English more often than not, though Weber liked to call it "English beyond remedy." Although he never mentioned the school except in such deprecatory ways, he had stayed there for four years. Sinclair knew he had not even applied for any sort of university teaching, although he was qualified for it. It was odd because Weber had never been the world-redeeming type and Sinclair thought it was odd too that whatever feeling he maybe did have for the place only came through, in some rerouted fashion, in the karate class, where all feeling was suppressed or at any rate transformed into something other than what it originally had been.

It was a chilly March day in East Harlem and Sinclair pulled a knit cap down to his eyebrows as soon as they got to the street. Weber hesitated on the steps of the school, letting a gusty wind whip his hair back and forth across his face. Since practice he'd been silent and quite thoroughly withdrawn.

"What would you say to a drink?" Sinclair said.

"Hello," said Weber. "I guess."

"Up here or downtown?"

"Down," Weber said with a crooked grin. "I've had my fight already for the day."

They caught the IRT coming into the station and rode to 86th Street in the rush hour press. Across the block from the stop there were two Irish railroad bars side by side. Bantry's was full of an after-work crowd so they went into Clancy's, where it was quieter. Clancy's was dark and narrow and smelled of corned beef and cabbage and the perpetual stale smell of beer. Sinclair and Weber got seats at the bar. Two glasses of beer were set up and Weber asked for a shot of vodka, tossed it off, and called for another. Sinclair blinked. Weber could drink — plenty. But usually he didn't go after it quite so hard right after practice.

Sinclair ordered a shot of bourbon for himself and drank it slowly. By the time he was done Weber had had four vodkas and two beers. He was shut off, away in some private reverie, looking into the mirror behind the bar, though it didn't seem probable to Sinclair that he actually saw anything reflected there. Sinclair had to look in the mirror himself to see Weber's set expression, and the sight of it next to his own puzzled face made him quite uncomfortable.

"Look," Sinclair said. "If you got away with it, you were automatically right. That's the final proof, isn't it?"

"Sure," Weber said in a joyless tone, and ordered another vodka. He didn't seem nearly as drunk as he should have. The thing about Weber, Sinclair recalled, was that he never did seem drunk until he keeled over sideways.

"You gambled and you won," Sinclair said, coming to the conclusion that it would be just as well for him to forget his private reservations about the whole episode for the moment. "You hustled a hustler. Why not feel good about it, right?"

Weber picked up one of the empty glasses in front of him and examined the bottom of it closely.

"Look," Sinclair said. "Okay, I'm sorry I rode you about it back at the school. I would just . . . It would be okay with me if you didn't take such big chances. It could have been done another way. But maybe I would have done it that way myself if it had been me."

"That's all right," Weber said. "That didn't bother me. I know it's a debatable point. At best, from my side of it."

"Well," said Sinclair. "You don't happen to want to eat anything, do you? Keep drinking that way on an empty stomach and you're going to fall on the floor before we ever get out of here. Right after a workout, too."

"I can live with that," Weber said.

"Hell," Sinclair said. He was still tingling from the practice, and as usual a bit sore here and there, and when he got up he could feel the bourbon he'd had all the way to his feet. "Suit yourself." He went to the steam table opposite the bar and after glancing over all the pans he had the waitress make him up a roast beef sandwich on a hard roll with a lot of mustard on it. Then he carried the plate and a salt shaker back over to the bar.

"Want half?" he said, sitting back on his stool.

"No," Weber said. "Thanks. I'm not trying to be a martyr or anything. I just want to get drunk, that's all."

"You're going about it the right way, then, I'd say."

"You're pretty good at it yourself, aren't you? You should know."

Sinclair laughed and Weber appeared to relax a little.

"It's not that guy up there," Weber said. "It isn't that at all."

"Well, why don't you tell me something about it? I can keep quiet if that's what you're worried about."

"I know you can," Weber said. "It's Marian."

"Oh." Sinclair chewed on the end of his sandwich. He had always had a low-key and largely unrequited taste for Marian's cousin and best friend, a comparatively quiet girl named Gwen, but he had mixed feelings about Marian herself. She could be charming, even wonderful at times. But she gave Weber fits, and Sinclair had to be loyal to Weber whenever those kind of chips were down.

"It's not the usual," Weber said. "She's pregnant."

Sinclair pushed his shot glass over the little lip on the inside of the bar and beckoned to the bartender to fill it up again. He paid for the drink and drank it and on reflection asked for another beer.

"What are you doing about it?"

"I'm not exactly being consulted," Weber said.

"Oh really?"

"She wants to . . . She says she's going to have an abortion."

"Well, now —"

"*No. Goddammit.*" Weber swayed. He was beginning to show the liquor, which meant, as a rule, that the clock had been started on his consciousness.

"It's absolutely, positively yours?"

"Yes. I mean, the way she's acting she's not exactly going to make a big point of it. But she hasn't said it isn't, either, and she probably would and I haven't got any reason to think it's not. But it's none of my business anyway, according to her. She's just going to have an abortion and that's it. She could have had it today for all I know."

"That bad, is it?"

"Looks permanent, at the minute."

"Oh hell, Weber, I'm sorry."

"I just can't hack it this way, this time. It's the piece not to eat, you know?"

"Listen. Try not to take this the wrong way, all right, but I don't think she's exactly ripe for motherhood at the moment, somehow."

"You think I don't know that?" Weber made a sudden move and wobbled on his stool.

"Take it easy, now."

"The abortion is not exactly the problem here. I haven't joined Right to Life or anything, not that it thrills me either."

"What would you do, then?"

"It's hard to say. First, we'd have a conversation, like maybe I had something to do with what happened at all, and then . . . I don't know. I don't know if we could get married or live together or anything like that. Could I take a kid myself? Probably we'd just do what she's doing, right? But it's wrong the way we're getting to it, it's wrong, that's all. I can't back off of it either this time. I can't. But she came out on the fire escape and screamed me all the way down the street —"

"Okay. I'm getting the picture."

Sinclair picked up a crust from his roll and looked at it and put it back down amidst the crumbs and gristle on the plate. He was going to be good and late for what he'd had planned next, but it didn't seem to matter so much now.

"She had one a little after we met," Weber was saying. "That could have been mine too, probably was, though it wasn't dead sure that time, it seems."

"And?"

"I don't know. I didn't care. Or something. I mean, I worried about *her* and everything. But the thing itself didn't seem to matter. But this one's very different."

"Try not to let it eat you, Weber. If she wants it to be all her problem, then it just will be, that's all. Could you try to look at it like that?"

"I have. But it doesn't look very good like that. In fact that's one of the worst ways it looks."

Weber drained off his glass of beer.

"She told me it was her second one, too," he said. "Back

there when I first met her. She'd had another one before. Before I knew her."

"It must get kind of hard on her."

"Not that she'd ever admit it in a million years. Third time's the charm, eh?"

"I'm not going to tell you I know how you feel."

"I wouldn't."

"Better not drink any more, Weber. You have to stop thinking about it all for a while. Or just go home." Sinclair knew that if Weber got just a little more maudlin in front of him he would have a hard time forgiving him later on for having witnessed it. He gave him a little punch on the arm.

"Don't torture yourself. Sounds like you've done what you can."

Weber raised his head from where it had been ducked between his elbows on the bar. He gave himself a shake and his eyes cleared a little.

"I could have killed that guy today, you know."

Sinclair shrugged. "He was a pretty bad guy anyway. Probably no great loss."

"But you don't get to kill people like that. You just don't. The whole thing was avoidable. I should never have put him with Carleton. I could have seen it coming."

"There you've got a point. Black suit usually means 'out for blood' if I'm remembering right."

"Yeah, I knew that, of course. I think I wanted it to happen all along, in a way."

"Well, you've got a right to feel bad about it, if that's really the truth. But don't be too hard on yourself. It could have been a hell of a lot worse. You handled it okay in the end."

"By dumb luck is how I handled it."

"I wouldn't say that. It was a risky technique. But it did work. You broke some of his ribs for him, I think, the way he was acting when he got up."

"I hit him with everything I had. I didn't know if he was ever going to get up or not and I don't think I cared. God, it felt so good to feel that contact. Even hitting the floor, and I banged hell out of my shoulder too . . . I wanted him dead. I did. Or me, or Marian, or the baby . . . Jesus, I don't know."

Sinclair thumbed his chin, uneasy.

"Weber. Don't fight again when you feel that way. Not *anybody*."

"Don't worry. Today was a close enough call for me too. I was out of control and I know it now."

Sinclair thought of having another drink and decided against it. Time to set a good example.

"I'll tell you a secret," he said. "Nobody can be in control all of the time."

"I know that. But it's hard. I don't see where it's going to get any easier for a while either." Weber made an ambiguous gesture and tumbled over a row of empty glasses. The bartender stood up, but when Sinclair signaled him he sat back down.

"Ah, Weber . . ." Sinclair began.

"All right," Weber said. "I got it. Could you maybe find me a cab somewhere, Jimmy? I think I succeeded to get drunk and everything. I doubt I'd make it home walking."

"I doubt you'd make it to the door," Sinclair said. "I can split a cab with you."

"I got it bad this time," Weber said. "All the time, too. I

wake up every morning and feel like I just took a fantastic kick in the liver."

Sinclair stood up and steadied Weber with a hand on his shoulder.

"You'll whip it, man. You will if you have to." Then he thought of something. "So what if you can't take it nose to nose. You'll just have to outsmart it then, that's all. Okay?"

"Right," Weber said tonelessly as a dead man talking. Sinclair took his hand away. He thought Weber was drunk enough to sleep when he got home, and there was certainly something to be said for that. It was going to be a rough time for Weber, clearly, and it was probably in his nature to make it harder than it had to be. Sinclair had not really been thinking much when he had said that thing about control. But now he understood that the remark was true, though it probably hadn't helped Weber all that much. For sure he probably hadn't helped Weber much with anything he'd said, but he believed he'd done all he could for the moment. That was a form of control too, wasn't it? In the slow motion of his mind's eye Sinclair saw again how hard and fast Weber had been able to strike back from his position on the floor. It wasn't a particularly pleasant image, and Sinclair tried not to think about it as he pulled the watch cap back down over his head and went out on the windy street to find a cab.

THE
NUMBERS
GAME

"I HATE MY JOB," I say. Just barely aware I'm saying it at all or even thinking it again. It's a phrase that pops up a lot, along with minor irritations. Like now, when Benton has just snatched the car around a corner a thousand times too fast, and for no reason either, just to flex a little muscle. Spilled my coffee, scalding hot coffee I just picked up for him and me. All down my pants leg. A big burning wet spot now on the blue cloth and when it dries there'll be that brownish crust from the cream. Trivial, but . . .

"Hang in there, kid," says Benton. "Only fifteen more years and you can start to draw your pension."

"Such a funny man," I'm mumbling. But Benton isn't listening anymore. To me, that is. His ears are pricked toward the radio, which has just buzzed out a 10-22. Mugging, I don't catch the address. Benton pulls down the sun visor where his score sheet is taped and makes a check mark on one of the columns. With the car just rolling along at will, of course.

"Watch the street, will you? You'll get us in another wreck." But Benton's not attending. His bullet head's sunk down in his limp collar, heavy lips moving a little, he's calculating.

"Was that ours?" I say. And I take a pull of what's left of my coffee. It's shallow enough now, anyway, it probably won't slosh anymore. The sourness of it already rising back in my throat. Well, I didn't have to pay for it at least. *I hate my job.*

"Oh yeah," Benton says. "It's ours." He flicks on the dome lights and gives the siren one good crank to bull his way through a left turn against the traffic of a Broadway intersection. Then he shuts off the special effects and drives downtown at a moderate pace, double-parking on the west side of the street, near 106th. The citizen's waiting for us in an all-night coffee shop around there. About the last place open on the block, being that it's now four A.M. approx. *Goddamn late shift.* Usually we'd be swing, but not tonight.

"Be nice and button up," I say to Benton, who's got his tunic undone over a yard of greasy gray undershirt. Sure it's a warm night, but still. Bad P.R., which has always been a problem with Benton. Even though he's senior to me. He'll let me talk him out of it sometimes, so I go first into the coffee shop while he's covering up the damage. The citizen's a bit overexcited and drunk too, looks like. White male thirty to thirty-five approx five nine one eighty madras sport jacket white shirt open collar no tie . . .

"Can you describe the perpetrator?" I say. I get to recite all this boilerplate because Benton has six years more on the force and is even sicker of it all than me. Under provocation he'll make fun of the citizens, and some of them have enough on the ball to call up the precinct and complain about him. Which usually means both of us, in terms of the total effect.

But this citizen is running down all the stuff he lost. Not just the wallet but rings and an engraved watch and I don't know what else. A diamond-studded I.D. bracelet or some such stupid thing. Can tell from his speech and manner he's from out of town. A conventioneer or something useful like that. Wants to know where he can go to get his stuff back.

"I'm sorry, sir," I say, "but I have to warn you that articles lost in these circumstances are very rarely recovered." Never, in fact. "Of course, if we get a good description and an early arrest . . ."

That's enough to change the subject, and I want to get done with this one. I like my gin better in a glass than on some citizen's breath. His would flatten an elephant. Benton's made it inside now, but he's not paying much attention. He's sitting at the counter drinking a glass of milk. The switchover to this tour always gives us both a rotten stomach.

Okay, the perp was a black male, had hair in cornrows or maybe it was dreadlocks, a white T-shirt or possibly a tan safari jacket, armed with a handgun or said he was . . . Basically this citizen does not really know what hit him. He was walking, crawling maybe, through the park across the street on his way from the Third Phase back to his buddy's apartment when suddenly —

"You're walking through that *park*, for chrissake?" Benton says, tuning in all of a sudden. The park's tiny, just a triangle in the middle of the intersection really, but there's a lot of shrubbery and Benton does have a point. "You couldn't cross over the street to where there's some lights and people maybe? At four o'clock in the freaking *morning?*"

"Yeah?" says the citizen, he's all ruffled up now. "With you on the beat a man don't feel safe in his own bed yet."

Out of town, definitely. A long jagged smile spreads along Benton's face from ear to ear. With no neck and the plug head he's got, this smile makes him look like a gigantic shark. Only a shark with a milk mustache.

"Drunk and disorderly," Benton says. "Write him up."

"Now, now, have a heart," I say. I have to be the one that makes nice too, another feature of my role when this kind of thing comes up. "The man's a little excited, maybe, he's just been robbed, remember."

This all helps the citizen calm down enough to tell me his name and address without any more bitching or complaint. Somewhere in Metuchen, that's where he's from.

"We'll let you know when we have an arrest," I say, shutting up my notebook. "Or if we recover your property."

"Don't call us," Benton says as he gets up. NC for the milk, I notice. Though this isn't one of our regular spots. *Our pleasure, ossifer.* In a pig's ear. "We'll call you."

"Another freaking unsolved mystery," Benton says, sniggering a little. I'm driving now, back uptown, then cutting across Cathedral Parkway.

"Oh, I love it, man, you always deliver just what we need," I tell him. "That guy will drop a dime on us for sure. Bright and early tomorrow morning. If not before."

"Nah, Braxton, you worry too much," Benton says. Still

with that big shark smile spread over his face. "He'll forget. He wouldn't know who to call anyway, a hick like that. A hick from the sticks, my boy. Besides which he *was* drunk and disorderly."

"Miss Pollyanna Benton," I say. "You'll be smiling out the other side of your mouth when Grigson starts biting on our tail over besmirching the good name of New York's Finest out in the provinces there . . . What've you got to be so cheerful about, anyway?"

"I'm ahead on the spread, my man," Benton says. "To-morrow morning I'll be a rich sumbitch. Gimme that sheet." I pull the paper down from the visor and hand it to him. Benton fondles it for a minute or so and then folds it up in his pocket.

"Still almost two hours to go," I say. Benton only grunts to that.

Okay, cruising up the wrong side of Morningside Park. It's a real forest of law enforcement opportunity in there. But nothing that particularly strikes my fancy. A wasteland of junkies and winos and rapists and thrill killers and things like that. It's dark in there. Can barely see across the edge of it from the car. Near 116th Street there's some Rasta types around a trash can fire. Could vag them probably, but not much point in it.

"10-23," the radio croaks. That's a guy out on a ledge somewhere. Not so near us, though, and already I hear the crackle and whine of another car responding. Somewhere back over there in yup town where people still have the leisure and inclination to kill themselves. Over here it's un-necessary. Too many people running around perfectly willing to take care of that for you.

"Oh baby, I got it taped," says Benton. From the corner of my eye I see him mark another column on his tally sheet and then start scratching figures.

"Betting heavy on suicide tonight, are you?" I say. "Don't you think that's a little morbid?"

The numbers game that Benton plays is not the kind you get collared and sent to the walls for. Just a sort of precinct pool. You bet on the radio call numbers, which mostly stand for different kinds of crime. Murder, rape, robbery, and on down. The works. Since statistics can predict which order the leaders are going to fall in, you don't bet your number to win, place, or show. You have to bet the spread *between* the categories. Then certain rare numbers like *officer down* or *hostage in the house* work sort of like double zero in roulette. Actually it's even more complicated than that. Which is one reason I don't play. Enough guys do to make it interesting, though. Benton understands it all, and he even has a certain knack for calling the spreads. Often he's as good an index as the dispatcher's computer. It's a kind of sixth sense he's got at times, or second sight.

A little insensitive? Sure it is.

"Ah, Braxton, you should of gone ahead and went to college," Benton says. "You're too freaking delicate to be a cop."

Benton does trust me, though. I know this by circumstantial evidence. We've been partners for two years and if he didn't trust me he'd of had me transferred the hell out of his car. But what he calls "delicate" has kept him out of a whole bucketful of trouble. Benton has always been a good cop, but also a troublesome cop. He's still low on the sergeant's list in spite of the drawerful of citations he's got. Aside from sassing the citizens, which is not really too serious of a setback, he's had two boards for shooting off his gun in not exactly the right circumstances. He smacked up our car pretty bad once, and nobody likes that much. And in 1978 he punched some guy that brought a civil suit.

Except for the wreck, all that was before they put me in his car. I'm a regulation cop. A goody-two-shoes. Still follow Police Academy rules, some of them anyway, after five years on the street. Benton likes to kid me about it, of course. But otherwise he'd be up before discipline every couple of months or so. As it is, the only bad thing he's done lately is break the arm of an underage pickpocket. I wasn't standing close enough to stop that one. But somehow it never got reported on him anyway.

So, "too delicate"? The hell you say. Only I just keep driving. Since I don't feel much like arguing tonight. Or like being a cop, either. If the truth is told.

"Nice kid like you from Forest Hills." Benton would really like to get my goat, I guess. I know his stomach's bothering him. He himself comes from the Bronx, though from one of the good neighborhoods. Probably nicer than Forest Hills, as a matter of fact. But the thing to do is ignore it. I've circled all the way back around to Eighth Avenue now. It's a warm night. One of the first hot nights of this spring. In spite of how late it is there's still people all over the street over here. I kind of have to be careful so I don't flatten some jaywalker in the dark. Little kids they got walking around here at almost five in the morning. Four-year-olds with the house keys pinned to their sleeve.

Well okay, goddammit, so I am a nice kid from Forest Hills. I even got into Music and Art when I was fourteen. Went two years but never liked it. Missed my friends and my own nabe. So I quit and came back. Dragged my feet and let my grades slide down. When I did the Police Academy instead of college I think it might of been mostly to bug my parents. That, and I thought it would be exciting, I guess. It was, too, for the first couple of years. Not the fun kind of excitement, exactly. More what you get from being frightened and confused all the time. Day after day after day.

Maybe Benton is right. *I hate my job.* Then *whammo,* I'm stomping on the brakes before I know exactly what this is I don't want to hit. Before I've really seen anything, for sure. I'm braced for the stop but Benton gets thrown up against the dash.

"What the —" He rocks back, collecting himself, and I see his left hand fall on the stock of the short little shotgun that rides in a holster between us, right over the transmission. A different kind of reflexes than I got. Fight or flight . . . There's two rail-thin arms punched into the hood and a head of tangled hair tossing above them. On the sidewalk a few heads are turned our way but only for a glance. Nobody really interested. I roll down the window.

Hispanic female in a pink tank top, white shorts going gray. Thin, very thin, breastless, I could count her ribs. Could be a junkie, only I don't see tracks on either of those wasted arms, propped on the top of the car door now. Impossible to say how old she is. And no way yet to ask a question. I'm supposed to speak Spanish, my occupational specialty. But it's bad high school Spanish and this lady's hysterical.

"Señora," I say. "Señora." And another badly framed phrase or two. Wine on her breath. I glance down at her knobbly knees. Little purple jail tattoos crawl up her legs like flies.

When she has to stop for breath she catches some of my mumbling and switches over to English. I don't get my feelings hurt over that anymore. Makes things easier, besides. She's a little incoherent still. But bit by bit I get the story. A lost kid, a daughter. Where? Somewhere in the tenement across the street. On information and belief. Where, as I get it, bad people live.

I take out my notebook and jot down some doodles. Because I'm slithering out from under this one. Not much interested in lost children, in fact. Not on this particular block, anyway. Most of the time they're only mislaid. Or else they're chips in somebody's domestic dispute. Never want in on those if you can help it. On dispatch we'd have to pursue it. Otherwise, I think not.

"How old?" I say.

"Six."

I draw a circle on my pad. Then a triangle, which I shade with slanted lines. As an afterthought, the numeral six.

"We'll look into it," I say.

The woman backs off a little from the car. Seems unlikely she'd satisfy that easy, but maybe something distracted her. Then I feel Benton's thumb in my ribs. I look over. His hand's back on the gun stock. Funny how he'll do that whenever something's going on. I've heard he was in Vietnam. Never from him, though.

"Let's do it."

"You're kidding, right? You know what time it is?"

"Sure I do."

"That whole building must be asleep."

"So? We can do it. Wake a few people up a little maybe."

Okay. I do actually know what he's got in mind. Practically the first call I was ever on was a lost child. A kid that was beamed up into outer space from the corner of Prince and West Broadway. Disappear from there and you definitely can get some cops. I wasn't Benton's partner then but we worked the buildings in groups of four and he was in the other car. It was really stupid, knocking on doors all day. But Benton did know how to play it for points. Not one to waste a free foot in anybody's door. And in fact he did get a few arrests out of it. Mostly cocaine, since it was SoHo. I believe he might have flushed a fugitive too. Never did find the kid, though. Nobody did, not to this day.

So Benton's way of thinking is, if you turn over enough rocks something awful is going to crawl out eventually. Then you can step on it. If that's what you like. Me, I don't mind if it just stays where it is.

"This ain't SoHo."

"Ah, c'mon, Braxton. It's a lost *kid*, chrissakes. Think of the benefit of humanity."

"Tell me about it, why don't you. I hear they're gonna canonize you any day up here."

That's a low blow, but I'm a little annoyed. Also that last coffee gave me heartburn. Benton's not so popular in these nabes since he broke the arm of the boy pickpocket. The odd thing is it's all over the place, not concentrated anywhere. Nothing very extreme either. Every so often a real dirty look, or somebody spits on the sidewalk after he passes. Since they can't really tell us apart I get the benefit of most of it too. But it's better than a civil rights suit any day. At least I think it is.

"Okay, now," Benton says. His voice gets low and frosty when he's mad. "Let's do it to it."

He pulls at the shotgun and I push it back down.

"Uh-uh," I say. "You know the order." The order is that the department doesn't want any shotgun to come out of a car unless there's a riot or a war. Not so long ago an unpleasant thing happened with a shotgun. Which is still in court and on the news. And for working this particular area, I agree with the department. Display a shotgun here and now, and people are going to think bad thoughts.

Benton stares at me. Our hands are touching on the gun butt and that makes me feel funny. "10-15," says the radio. Then, "10-23."

"Some more good news for you, Benton," I say. To break the tension. Benton doesn't act like he heard me. But then he drops his eyes.

"Okay, then," he says. And lets go of the gun.

Then he gets out of the car. I see the woman dart over to him and start jabbering again.

Damn it. I never thought he'd go without the shotgun. Now there's nothing I can do but go with him. They're all the way to the tenement door there. I see their shadows against the hall light. She's getting worked up again. Waving her arms. *Damn it to hell.* I pull out my gun and snap out the cylinder to check the load. A little luxury, this gun. Not the regular service item but a Ruger .357 mag. With a four-inch barrel too. Unlike a lot of cops I do time and to spare on the range. It took me months to learn how to handle the recoil on this cannon. But now it'll hit whatever I aim it at, nine times out of ten. Never pointed it at anything but a paper target, though, and hope I never will. I put it back in the holster. Pound my chest where that sour gas bubble is stuck. I reach over to lock Benton's door and then I get out and lock mine.

·　　·　　·

Later, an hour or so later when it's all over I will be thinking, *There.* That was the last moment when I could have done something different, or maybe something could have happened to make it all come out different after that.

We're to the third floor now and not much to show for it either. Forty-five minutes or so of door-knocking. Benton's edged his way into a couple of apartments he thought felt right. But his instinct seems to be on the blink. Haven't even turned up a Mexican joint. All we've accomplished so far is bad public relations. The building's waking up now, the two floors below us. Doors banging, the odd voice calling up and down the hall. A big amount of swearing in two languages. Whole place is buzzing like a hive. Makes me a little nervous.

"Let's bag it," I say to Benton, slogging into the fourth floor hall. The stairwell circuit's blown, or someone stole the bulbs. Ink black going up, but at least the halls are lit. A little. It's a weird effect.

"Nah, gotta finish," Benton says. Gotta for what? He moves to the first door on the hall. There's four apartments to the floor. The hall's narrow. Almost have to walk sideways, it feels like. Crummy brown plaster walls written over with gang slogans and sex pictures. And a thick smell of wine and urine. The place is an open toilet.

Pound pound pound, goes Benton on the door. I come up behind him, can hear the slow dragging of feet. It's taking a long time.

"Police officers," Benton calls, shifting his weight. All up and down the hall people must be hiding their guns and dope, I'm sure. The door cracks open, on the chain. Here's the tiniest little old black lady in the world. Hair dead white and over her eyes the cloudy blue film of cataracts. No wonder it took her a while to get to the door.

"Who?" she says. "Who?"

"Oh, go back to bed, little mama," I say. "Benton, for God's sake."

Benton steps back and lets the door bump shut. But he won't look at me. He heads for the door all the way at the end of the hall. Well, at least it looks like he might be planning to skip a couple.

Bam bam bam, Benton goes on the door. A pause. Then his body ripples like a dog pointing, and I see him raise one finger. I go toward him, setting my feet down carefully, quietly. Benton gives me a look, eyes crinkled at the edges with attention. And I know what he means. Can feel it myself. That door, the room behind it, is listening just as hard as we are.

Bam bam bam, goes Benton's fist. "Police." A few more seconds of that weird silence. Then, *crash*. And again, *crash*. Benton and I trade another glance.

"Open up," he says. And I don't exactly hear anything but I perceive that something is approaching the other side of the door. Then, right there in the door plate, there's a little click. Hell, I think, the door must of been open all the time and now he's just locked it. I reach out for the knob to try it.

"Let's open on up, now," Benton says, and as my fingers close around the knob the door whips open and snatches me with it. It's dark and something very heavy and hard slams me across the back and shoulders with enough power I almost tap out. I fall forward, tucking in my shoulder to roll — they teach you this in Police Academy — and come up on my knees. I see Benton fold over, something big and blurry has just clobbered him with the same thing, whatever, that hit me, and I reach for the Ruger. Can't find it, *no*, now I've got it. Can't think of any words, not *stop* or *freeze*, just a kind of yelp that gets the perp's attention.

The guy is big, huge, seems like there's no end to him. Tissue straining at itself all over him. A body that's been loved and worked on. He's a body builder, or else just a natural monster. His legs're a bit short and bowed, and I see he's barefoot, why we didn't hear him coming. His head's kind of small, sunk down between those shoulders. What I'll never forget is how pretty that face is: black wavy hair, long eyelashes, a little snub nose and lush cherry mouth. A girl's face grafted where it doesn't belong. I know I'm going to remember it and see it and keep on seeing it long after it's time for that to stop.

I see now what he's got is a hatchet. In his hands it looks like a toothpick. But I had one like it when I was a Boy Scout at eleven. So I know it's a foot long and heavy and sharp and dangerous. I'm wondering how much damage he's done with it just now when he throws it at me, I duck, he runs.

"Stop," I shout. "Hold it." I remember how to talk again, standing up in the doorway. But he's not about to stop. The hall seems longer now. So I have time to do it by the book. Set my feet apart. *Think triangle*. Both hands on the gun, pulling it down an imaginary plumb line through the middle of his back.

"Last chance," I'm yelling. *Squeeze, don't jerk.* He doesn't stop, almost to the stairs now. Everything drags like a slow-motion movie, even with subtitles running across the bottom of the picture that say, *I hate my job*, and then, *I quit.* He swings around the bannister to the right, and squeezing the trigger I pull the gun a little to the left, just to make sure, and see a foot-wide hole open in the lath and plaster well before I notice the crash and whine. Now there's nothing over there but hunks of plaster tumbling out of the edges of the hole, and the sucking darkness of the stair-well.

Jesus Christ, that hatchet . . . I start reaching back and feeling all over myself. No place wet, I don't think I'm bleeding. Just the beginning of a fantastic welt and bruise. He must of been using the hammer end. On Benton too. He's sitting up. Not showing any blood either. I crouch down by him.

"G-guh-god*damn.*" Okay, I see it's not fatal.

"I'll go down and call it in," I say. "Somebody might could still pick him up. A crazy weightlifter roaming around barefoot."

But Benton grabs at my arm. Hasn't got his wind back enough to talk. Just keeps shaking his head.

"Well, why not?" I say. He lifts his head and looks at me. And I know he saw it then. And he knows I know he knows.

When we check out the apartment it's dead empty. Somebody moved out and nobody moved in. There's two smashed places in the kitchen wall I think might go with the two crashes we heard. The perp was practicing, I guess. For us . . . And that's it. Not a mattress. Not a toothbrush.

Nothing to hide or protect. Just one of those senseless things.

Back in the car I say to Benton, "Now?" He won't even turn my way. Just a dead-fish stare over the wheel and out along the street. The night's turning blue already. The days're getting longer.

"Look," Benton says. "What's the point. The guy's long gone. You'd only have to write up all that paper on your gun. Better off if you skip it."

So. We both sit there. Daylight's leaking down the street, washing over the buildings. Finally it's quiet around here, and no one's out. *I quit, man, I quit.* Funny how I feel all ragged about it, even though the main thing's really relief. I should of blown the guy away. It wasn't altogether justified, no. But close enough for rock and roll. I can picture it, what it would have been like. That mag shell put a hole in the wall big enough for a dog to jump through. Well. Now I know. It occurs to me that lots of guys probably don't find out before they're dead.

Snap crackle pop, goes the radio, spitting up more numbers. That brings Benton back to life. He pulls out his tally sheet and starts going over it. That's a longer way from me now than it ever was before, isn't it though. Benton can beat the odds if he can. And welcome to it. From here on out, what I hope for is not to end up in the wrong column. Myself personally, that is. Benton's smiling a little to himself. I figure he's still ahead but I'm not going to ask him. We don't really have to ask each other questions now. It might take a week, two weeks, to make it all official. But I've already quit back up there on that hall. I know it and Benton knows it too.

Now the radio's talking about some missing persons report. An address back over on Broadway somewhere. Sounds like jive to me. Some Barnard chick forgot to call home and got her mama all bent out of shape. Then Benton picks up the handset and answers the call.

"What?" I say. "Why, there's only fifteen minutes left to this shift, we could be turning in the car." He doesn't answer, and I don't push it. Just sit back and watch the street slide back behind the car. Fifteen more minutes, thirty, what the hell.

106th and Broadway. We're putting in our time on this block this tour. I follow Benton in. One of those big old run-down lobbies. I wait by the creaky elevator in the back while Benton goes to find the super and comes back with passkeys. The elevator's a long time coming. When we get in it I feel like a coffin lid just shut down on me. I look up at the warped mirror in the corner. That's no relief. Sweat is starting to pop out all over my face and the hollow of my throat. Oh, I know what it is, all right. Some time after you've been under fire the shock is going to wear off. Then you get the fear and the panic. It can be an hour or a day. I've been warned about it. But now that doesn't seem to help. I'm so dizzy I have to sit down on the floor.

Up above me I see all that heavy cop stuff hanging off of Benton's belt. The ticket book and cuffs and gun and all the other gear I carry too. Why, if only I took off my belt I'd probably be able to stand up again. Sure I could. I'd be so light I'd float like a feather.

Now the elevator doors come open, though I see we've hit the wrong floor. Benton kneels down beside me.

"Hey," he says. "What gives, kid, need a little air?" Ben-

ton can be a real bastard a good part of the time, and he is.
But on occasion I've seen him turn very patient and kind.
If a citizen is really hurt or in bad trouble. I know he doesn't
act that way to anyone that has his full respect. But now I'm
grateful for it just the same.

"Why?" I ask him. "What for?"

"What for, what?" Benton says. His hand is gentle on my
pulse.

"Why'd you want to take this call? We could of went to
the station."

Benton laughs a little.

"That's all's bothering you? Well," he says. "It's a 10-23.
I need it to fill in my bingo card. Otherwise it might get
listed on the next shift."

"But it was a missing person."

"That's what they think it was."

"You can't know that."

"But I do. Look," Benton says, and he tightens his grip on
my wrist. "Can't you feel it?"

And I do. I do feel it. Cold turning, a shadow in the house.
Who in hell would want to be able to feel things like that?
I pull my arm loose and get up.

"It's just a feeling," Benton says. It's the first time I ever
heard him sound like he was puzzled by something. "It's
kind of hard to explain." Then he stands up too.

"You okay? Feel better?"

"No problem," I say. "Sorry I faded out on you." I'm not
faking it, either. Now I don't feel anything but tired. "Let's
go on up."

Benton hits the elevator button and the doors hiss shut.
He's talking more now. Explaining how it's normal, what
just happened to me. Nice of him, okay. He won't have too

many more chances to do me any favors, and I'm sure he can see that almost as well as I can. But I can't stand to listen to him now. I shut my eyes and start talking to myself to block his voice out. It's almost like a prayer, I guess. *Be wrong, be wrong*, I'm thinking, but this time I know he's right.

HOUR OF LEAD

―――――――――――――――――――――――――

"**W**HAT THE HELL do you think all that is?" Weber was saying. They had got a little ahead of her and closed in together; Marian hated it when they did that. Of course, if she hadn't rubbed Weber so far the wrong way earlier he'd probably be more in the mood to walk with her now.

"Couldn't tell you," Sinclair said. "I mean, I don't know what the pretext could be." Way ahead on the far side of Canal Street they could all see festival lights strung high from the lampposts, arranged in swooping arches that receded north on Mulberry.

"San Gennaro?" Weber said.

"Not this time of year, is it?"

She was losing ground; Weber and Sinclair were barely in earshot now, though they tended to speak loudly on the street. It being a Friday night and not too cold, Chinatown was jammed with out-of-towners, going the wrong way for the most part and moving with all the vivacity of glue. A foggy-eyed family of five filled the sidewalk before her, wandering forward in an oblivious bovine way, and she stepped into a doorway to let them pass. Stoned on MSG, no doubt. The display case in front of her was full of the usual Oriental bric-a-brac; she registered a couple of ornamental pipes, a finger trap, two rows of laughing Buddha figurines, before her eyes fell out of focus and the shelves dissolved into a nonspecific glittering. She turned back to the sidewalk and leapt into an opening in the flow of passersby. Now she could see Weber's head and Sinclair's moving above the heads of others, almost a whole block ahead. She didn't want to lose them, not quite, but be damned if she'd yell at them to wait. As she was vigorously thinking this thought, she saw Weber stop and turn.

"*Marian!*" he was calling. That softened her a little. Weber hated to have to shout in the street. She could see his head turning back and forth like a radar dish, trying to home in on her. Marian tucked her chin in a moment, by reflex, and then lifted it again.

"All *right*," she called. "You can cool your jets, I'm coming."

Weber and Sinclair stood together waiting for her, and the swarming people broke and divided around them as Marian came up.

"What's the story up Mulberry Street?" Sinclair said. "Got any ideas?"

"Nothing beyond the obvious," Marian said. She fell in step between them as they started off again.

"And I thought you were a Catholic," Weber said. His tone was light but there was a twitchiness in how he kept looking at her and then back away.

"Ha," Marian said. "Well, call it the Feast of Saint Dymphna, then."

"Saint Dymphna?" Sinclair said.

"Saint Dymphna, the patron saint of nervous illness," Marion and Weber said, not quite in unison, but close. Sinclair's eyebrows rose and he let out a startled laugh. Marian and Weber remained sober. They had come to the corner of Canal Street, where the light was red. It was darker here than on the Chinatown blocks. A quantity of litter from the daytime street market was strewn westward down the slope, smelling heavily of fish. Across the way a line of painted plywood booths stretched back hissing and sputtering under the rows of arcade lights.

"I don't know," Weber said. "Catania'll probably be crowded."

"Well," Sinclair began. "We could always —"

"Don't worry about it," Marian said, "They'll all be in the street. Trust me, I've been around these things before." She timed a gap in the Canal Street traffic and sailed into it, the long tails of her black raincoat snapping at her heels.

On the other side of the street it wasn't good — too noisy, too bright. The sidewalks were overgrown and crawling with their load of parasitic activity. Marian walked down the precise middle of the street, holding herself equidistant from the booths on either side. She'd left the others behind now (Weber rarely trusted himself to jaywalk) and she regretted it a little. Although the small festival was not really very crowded, it rang and buzzed like the inside of a pinball machine. The fluorescent tubes lining the booths sprayed her with their harsh explosive light. Everything was covered with a thick greasy smell of roasting meat, as if it were a tangible film. Marian's stomach folded in three places and began to roll over and over. When Weber's arm settled gently around her shoulders she flinched, couldn't help it, she just flinched. He took his hand away fast enough, though she could see he still wanted to make the best of it, for the moment.

"Shall I win you a woolly bear?" Weber said, looking back and forth with a crooked smile. Sinclair had drifted to the side of the street to watch a game where people were tossing rings at stakes. Prizes hung from the upper frame of the booth, coated with livid primary-colored fuzz.

"They're awful," Marian said involuntarily.

"Well," Weber said. "Sure they are." His voice hardened as the sentence closed. "Maybe I could get you a sandwich, then? A nice sausage hero with tomato sauce all over it?"

"Oh, don't be nasty," Marian said.

"Why not?" Weber said. "Why should I have to be the only one? Can you tell me that?"

He looked at her through a brittle face and she turned quickly and walked ahead. After a moment she heard Sinclair's and Weber's voices taking up some conversation behind her but she did not focus on the words. Where was Catania, anyway? The festival had changed the shape of the block into something unfamiliar. No, it was on the next block.

"Oh," Sinclair's voice said happily. "Look at that. Guns."

Weber said something indistinct and both voices faded to a burr as Marian walked through the intersection. On this block the booths were more sparsely set, with gaps between to allow people to come and go from the cafés and restaurants. Here were repeated much the same food vendors they'd passed previously, the same ring game and wheel of fortune. Marian could no longer hear the others coming behind her, and when she looked over her shoulder she saw they had not crossed the street. For a moment she dithered on the spot and then went back to look for them.

Weber stood at the first booth below the intersection, watching Sinclair, who was bent over a little rifle which was fixed by a swivel to the booth. As Marian came to Weber, Sinclair's hand tightened and the gun spattered something brassy into the back of the booth with a sudden rattling noise. Sinclair straightened up and a boy with smooth black hair and a glossy lack of expression stepped from the rear to exchange a pair of long slim tubes in the barrel of the gun.

"How do you like that?" Sinclair said. "A BB machine gun."

Weber handed the boy a dollar and bent over the gun. Marian moved around the corner of the booth so she could see what they were shooting at. Paper targets about twice the size of playing cards were clipped to a cord in the back of the booth; on each was stenciled a small red heart. Weber squeezed the trigger and one of the targets began to twitch and shudder. A line of perforation crossed from its left edge and chewed at a portion of the heart in the middle. Then the gun clicked empty and Weber snapped his fingers and stood up.

"No, I get it," Sinclair said. "You've got to do it in short bursts. Like with a real one." He paid and lowered himself over the gun.

"What's the object here, exactly?" Marian said.

"Oh," Weber said. "Get rid of all the red. You've got to punch it out, see . . ."

Sinclair's shots came now in brief chattering clusters. His aim seemed to improve by small fractions.

"And then?" Marian said.

"They give you a fuzzy-wuzzy, I guess." Weber watched Sinclair as the boy passed him his torn target. Scraps of scarlet clung at the edges of the ragged hole in the center. Sinclair shook his head.

"Not quite as easy as it looks, as the saying goes."

Weber gave up another dollar bill.

"Ahem," Marian said. "This looks as if it could go on."

"Want a turn?" Weber said.

"I'd rather have a beer."

"Just a minute, then," Weber said.

"Well," Marian said. "You know where to find me."

"All right," Weber said, turning to the gun. "We'll be up."

"Boys will be boys, won't they?" Marian said, or maybe she only thought it. Sinclair waved to her with one finger as she started back up the block.

Catania was even quieter than she had expected it to be. The square tables stood empty on the black and white tiled floor. At one an old man of the neighborhood was dozing behind a pair of empty beer glasses. Even the owner wasn't in tonight, though his image looked down from two large portraits hung on either side of the absurdly tall grandfather clock on the rear wall. The ceiling here was double height and the fancy woodwork behind the bar climbed almost all the way to it.

Marian took a seat at the bar, near the door. Timothy was bartending but he hadn't seen her yet. The television was turned up crazily loud, and he was gazing up at it, his mouth slightly parted, so that the points of his front teeth could be seen. Though it was warm in the bar, he seemed to be wearing a number of sweaters over each other, as if to give his jacket a better purchase on his skeletal frame. He sat with the perfect stillness of a reptile, a bony hand splayed on the counter like a lizard's foot. Marian had thought him either slow witted or surly until she'd finally realized he was only very deaf.

"I'LL HAVE A BOTTLE OF BUD," she screamed at him. Timothy twitched as her words cut through, and darted to the cooler, a movement so abrupt it could hardly be noticed before it was complete. Marian shrugged out of her trench coat and brought it up to the bar. Timothy set down the wet bottle and a short tumbler before her. Marian hesitated.

"A shot of vodka too," she said, amplifying the phrase with a gesture understood between them. There was no one to complain about it, after all. She pulled out a ten from her purse and smoothed it on the bar while Timothy poured the drink. When he had turned to make change she knocked the shot back quickly and sipped from the brown bottle. Timothy pushed the change toward her and resumed his seat below the TV. Marian drank from the beer. The glue of the label had softened in the ice chest and she discovered that she could pull it off whole with her fingernails. A crescendo of screaming spread out from the television and she looked up. It was something to do with a big win of something. Lotto, she was just able to discern that. Someone's number had come in, in an important way. She shut her eyes to see bright-numbered wheels revolving.

Wheel of fortune. Carnival. The Feast of Saint Dymphna, *ha*. The vodka lay in her stomach, inactive as if she'd swallowed a pebble. She simply was not in a festival mood.

Shouldn't have come out, maybe. The mirror across the bar showed her that she looked good tonight, but that didn't raise her spirits much. She spread the beer label on the bar, not looking at it. Her eye caught the yellowing cardboard pregnancy warning taped to the mirror above the bottles and skated away. The television went on roaring.

Oh what the hell have a drink kiddo it's the best fun you'll *ever get out of this world best seize the day there will be no tomorrow* and she cut herself off by rapping the shot glass hard against the counter. When she told Weber there would be hell to pay, not that that would be quite the worst of it either. Timothy collected the price of the second drink from the little heap of singles on the bar and went back to the TV. She drained the little glass and now a solitary finger of warmth uncurled inside her, but it was a long way from touching her mind. You'd think on an empty stomach . . . She shut her eyes and recalled Sinclair threading his way through the tables to the pay phone at the back of Hao Shih Chieh and heard Weber hissing, "Why can't you eat a little something at least," and when she didn't answer, "What do you come out for if it's going to be like this," and then in a different tone, "I'm worried about you, that's all, for God's sake, don't you know that?"

"I didn't have anything else to do," she'd said, and Weber said, "Oh?" and she said, "I couldn't decide what to do," and he put a hand softly on her forearm because he really did have an idea what she meant by this. Weber didn't say "What's wrong?" but she could hear him thinking it and they might have got it over with then and there only here came Sinclair back from the phone, line busy, no answer, something like that. So it was still hanging over them and sticking to everything with the humidity of approaching bad weather.

"On the house," Timothy said. Marian blinked her eyes open to the refilled shot glass, liquid shivering at the lip. Timothy smiled.

"HERE'S TO YOU," she shouted, and picked up the glass and drained it with a smooth steady movement, not spilling any part of it. Timothy acknowledged her with a nod and went back to the television. Marian picked up her money, leaving a dollar on the bar, and went out and down the block with the loose bills folded over in her hand.

"I can't cut it," Weber said, fanning out a sheaf of punctured targets in his two hands. "I'm just not quite good enough to win you a woolly, babe."

"You're making a noble effort, though, aren't you," Marian said. Through the bend of Weber's elbow she could see Sinclair still concentrating on the stutter of his gun.

"Well, I just thought you might like a moment of solitude. A quiet little opportunity to get primed." Weber's mouth was tight at the corners. "Did you manage to get primed?"

Marian plucked one of the targets from the batch, as in pick-a-card-any-card. Almost all of the heart had been drilled away but there was a curl of crimson down at the lower edge where the design had come to a point. Solitary holes were scattered over the paper here and there at random.

"I almost had it with that one," Weber said. "That was one of my very best efforts of all."

Marian stuck a finger through the hole in the target and explored the shreds of paper around the edges.

"I can't get primed anymore, you know," she said, studying the movements of her finger. "It doesn't sink in, I don't know. It doesn't have any effect."

"Well, you're in sad shape, aren't you? Can't get drunk, can't eat, can't tell a person what the hell's the matter with you . . ." Weber stopped. "And you left your coat in the bar, didn't you. I better run check if it's still there."

"Don't, I can go —" Marian said, but he had already started quickly away. He didn't want to really lose his temper, she could see that. *Dammit I'm not so starved down I can't get pregnant anyhow how do you like that*, and the time was surely coming when she would have to say this aloud, too. Her finger tore through the hole in the target and it fluttered out of her hand to the ground. Wrapped around the fingers of her other hand were the bills she had left from the bar. She flipped the corner of one with her thumb, turned around to the booth, and grasped the stock of the gun. The little rifle felt foolishly light in her hand but it spoke with a kind of authority.

brrrdddttttit'smybody andmybusinessandnobodyelse'sbrr rdddtttyoucan'tkeepondoingthistoyourselfbrdddttttit'smyse lfandIcandowhateverIdecidetodotoitbrrrrdddttttt

The lower part of the target detached and swooped off toward the lower corner of the booth. The scrap still hanging from the cord was a bare fishy white.

"I did it," Marian said, straightening up.

"Ah, well," Sinclair said. "It seems they have a rule, you can't cut it all the way in two."

"Always something," Marian said.

"Not bad at all for the first try, though. You'll get it this time."

"No, I don't think . . ." Marian folded her two bills in thirds and pushed them down into her tight hip pocket.

"I'd better see where Weber's got to, he went to look for something for me."

Farther up the street it was darker than it had been a few minutes before. Some of the booths were beginning to close down, snapping off their lights and shuttering their doors. Marian saw Weber coming across the intersection with her raincoat folded across his arm. She went up to the corner and waited to meet him under the lamppost.

"Thanks," she said, reaching for the coat. "You didn't have to." Weber put a string into her hand and her fingers closed on it reflexively.

"I brought you a balloon."

Marian looked up. Somehow she'd failed to notice it as Weber crossed the street. It too was heart shaped, bulbous, with a silvery metallic sheen. It was buoyant enough to pull the cord plumb straight, but its upward pressure on her hand was very slight. Marian put her free hand on Weber's shoulder and drew herself up to kiss him on the corner of the mouth. Then she stepped back and without the least premeditation let go of the string. The balloon drifted back up the street and they both watched it go. It rose very slowly, at not much of an angle, trailing its string loosely along the wood roofs of the amusement stands on the opposite sidewalk. Every so often it caught a sparkle of one or another light and sent back a tinselly reflection. Then it swam into a patch of shadows and was gone.

Weber, who'd corkscrewed himself around to follow the balloon's lethargic flight, turned back to her now. He wasn't angry, she could see that well enough, but just worn out. They were standing close enough to touch. Some words were half formed in her mind but she couldn't quite complete their shape.

"Oh, Marian." Weber spoke first, almost with the cadence of a song. "I see you going down that lonesome road."

Marian pushed the door shut with a shoulder, dropped her keys, and in picking them up spilled a pair of oranges from the sack she held cradled in her left arm. She set the groceries on the hall table beside the telephone and chased the oranges farther down the hall to the studio door. Her short-heeled shoes clacked loudly on the bare hall floor. She dropped the oranges back in the sack and turned the deadbolt in the door, then picked up the big portfolio and carried it back down the hall to the studio.

The watch on her wrist said four but the light was still strong in the studio. Her drafting table was angled to catch the best of it, and on an adjacent flat table her protractors and her pens and inks were laid out at right angles to each other. Marian leaned the portfolio against the wall and went to the drafting table, setting her hip against the edge of the high stool. Clipped to the board was a little wash drawing, meant for an illustration to a children's book called *The Cherry Stone*. Marian touched a finger to her lip and then to certain places on the drawing which did not please her. The portfolio slipped and slammed against the floor and Marian cursed and went to pick it up. The clicking of her heels seemed to trail her at a short distance, like an invisible but devoted pet determined to follow every move she made. She kicked the shoes off, going back into the hall, then turned and retrieved them and carried them to the bedroom closet, where she set them into the orderly row of her other shoes. Ever since the necessary business she had been increasingly fetishistic about tidiness; perhaps it was going a little too far. The whole apartment was breathlessly clean and so neat that a sloppy thought might have deranged it.

Now the droop of the grocery sack on the hall table reproached her and she hurried to carry it to the kitchen. There were the fruit, two cheeses, a damp sack of sprouts, and at the bottom of the bag a cold cube of frozen diet dinners. All this she laid on the shelves of the refrigerator, and then on second thought took out an orange and got a blue plate from the cabinet and sat down at the kitchen table. She slipped her fingernail under the skin of the orange and carefully unwound it in a single piece. When she had done, the peel stood in a spiral, almost retaining the shape of the orange, not quite. Marian undid all the sections of the orange and spread them over the plate and looked at them. After a little time she took the peel and tore it into small scraps which she took to the living room and scattered over the radiator there. Back in the kitchen she covered the plate thoroughly with plastic wrap and opened the refrigerator to put it away.

Maybe she was getting a little lightheaded. Eating had seemed an increasingly insurmountable challenge ever since the necessary business had transpired. Weber would be nagging her if he were still around. Marian gazed into the refrigerator, admiring how perfectly cold and white it was in there . . . It struck her that probably the refrigerator wanted to be empty — the blotches of color and form that represented the food held it back from an ideal of emptiness.

The glitter of plastic and chrome came at her with a

piercing force. She banged the door shut hard enough to shake the whole unit and stalked into the living room, where she had to stop and straighten out an ashtray and a book which seemed to have drifted a little askew on the coffee table. This neatness kick was getting out of hand possibly, but once it got started it was hard to stop. Of course the whole thing with Weber had been messy enough for a lifetime, worse even than she'd predicted; they'd both been completely out of control.

Marian marched toward the bathroom, away from the memory. For some reason that was harder to not think about than the other, but then the other was really a nonevent, something that could have happened but didn't. She'd learned the mood could be broken if she stared at herself in the bathroom mirror for long enough; in time her identity would pour out of her and into the image — other and forever the same. She had stood there incalculably long the night the bleeding started again and didn't want to stop. The idea that people sometimes died in such a circumstance occurred to her distantly, like a piece of news on the radio when you weren't really listening, or a note addressed to someone else you glanced at by mistake. Then the empty-eyed face in the glass had parted its lips and spoken its single phrase.

Oh you.

That was it. In the morning she wasn't dead at all, just fine, empty and clean as a whistle. Only now she might be overdoing the tidiness bit, Marian thought, fingering the blue scarf she wore tucked into the throat of her blouse, mouthing words at her reflection: *Hey, lighten up, let yourself go.*

Okay. She snapped her fingers and walked down the hall to the studio. The natural light was going now, so she flicked on her lamps and adjusted them until the illumination on the drawing board was flat. From the high stool she peered down at the cherry stone picture. It was an ostensibly educational text which detailed the progress of the cherry stone from fruit to sprout to tree, a drab little parable which would have to ride on the illustrations if it ever went anywhere at all. In the drawing on the table the cherry stone hung in the interior of its fruit, with its features supposedly just beginning to form. Marian had wanted the face to look amusingly confused and had succeeded, she thought wryly, in making it look schizophrenic. She undid the scarf and fingered the fringed ends of it, then took up a drafting pen and began to crosshatch under the eyes of the cherry stone face, trying to soften its expression.

Then the cherry stone was beginning to look extremely depressed. Marian pulled the drawing off the board and on a fresh sheet quickly sketched a series of figures unrolling from a cherry-stonish sphere, just a few quick lines for each. When she had done they looked like little goblins, ripe with bad intentions. Sitting back, she abstractedly began to make little black dots on the inside of her wrist, the needle point piquing her flesh. An impulse came on her to stick the point all the way up under the skin, to make a mark that would really last. She capped the pen and laid it aside and stood up. It had got completely dark (she must have lost track of the time) and the man across the street was staring into the studio window, as he did whenever he had a chance. Marian pulled the scarf off her shoulders and snapped it in his direction, then walked over and pulled down the blind.

From a distance the new sketches didn't look much better. They would probably frighten any child small enough to engage with the moronic text. Marian drifted away from the drawing table, across the hall to the living room, where she stood in the middle of the floor, twirling the scarf.

All work and no play make Jill a dull girl, she hummed to herself, waving the scarf in front of her in little flirts and stoops. There were a few gold threads woven into the deep blue mesh. Marian took the scarf at the edges and pulled it so taut that she could see through it. *Time to have some fun*, she thought with sudden conviction.

She furled the scarf and wrapped it around her wrist. For a couple of weeks she'd been holed up, avoiding the phone, but that was a trend which could easily be reversed; there were thousands of people she could call. It had been ten days at least since she'd had anything even so exciting as a can of beer, and now the idea of assorted pleasures tingled through her with lively anticipation.

Okay, let's have a party. She whirled the scarf off her wrist and tossed it to the ceiling. It struck lightly, opened like a parachute, and settled with a whisper to the floor. *You better pick that up*, Marian told herself. Something in the way the scarf lay crossed over itself reminded her of a snakeskin. She had an abrupt impression that she must pick it up at once or else she never would. Stepping forward, she touched the scarf with her bare toe and it gave a shiver like a live thing. It would be the start of something if she let it lie there. Marian turned her back on it sharply and went down the hall to the telephone.

Little cubes and pyramids of light tumbled through the chinks in the curtains and struck different areas of her body with what seemed a palpable effect. She ought to do something about those curtains — though they were already as heavy and dark as could be obtained. Masking tape around the edges, maybe. That was a bit morbid, though. Marian lay on her back, running a thumb down the raveled edge of her blanket. She wanted to turn over but did not quite have the energy. Although she could not remember every moment of the night she was quite sure she had not slept at all. Her whole body was stretched with a wiry tension and a weary unrelenting consciousness. All night a headache had lain close beside her and she knew whenever she moved it would move too.

She rolled her eyes, trying to find a clock without moving her head, not succeeding. It would be seven or maybe eight o'clock. Beyond the thick curtains traffic ground up and down Broadway, an incessant screeching and lurching formed into a monolith of sound, as though the whole river of pavement and vehicles constituted a single agonized machine. Marian's eyes roamed the ceiling now, looking for some place to rest. She closed them and nausea started up like an animal awakening after hibernation. Not good. She opened her eyes and fixed them on the post at the lower left corner of the bed. The conviction came to her that the party was really over now.

Clenching herself together, she swung her feet to the floor and sat up. With this motion something seemed to roll forward just behind her eyes. When she stood she felt giddy and hollow, but no real pain came through yet, though she could sense it waiting somewhere near. Navigating the littered bedroom floor with care, she worked her way out to the hall and walked down to the bathroom. There was a full-length mirror attached to the back of the bathroom door and when she faced it she saw with a mild shock that she was naked.

The body was all composed of triangles now, from the point of her chin to the concave wedge between her thighs. All of its rondures were gone. She would do well to eat something, but that idea revolted her and she pushed it away. In the declivity just below the join of her ribs a patch of skin pulsed in and out: a regular galvanic twitch. Marian watched it dully; it did not really interest her but she found it hard to look away. There was a passage of time and then her head began to thud in the same pattern. Marian broke from the mirror and turned to the sink. The top was off the Tylenol bottle but when she snatched it up it gave a re-assuring rattle. She shook out four capsules and swallowed them one by one, bending to gulp cold water from the faucet. Now she began to feel how cold it was in the bath-room. The tiles were freezing under her feet. A hot bath. She twitched aside the shower curtain and found the tub somehow full of sodden newspaper and some other matter she had no real wish to identify. The shower curtain fell back in place. Her head continued to pound in the stout rhythm of her heart.

It might be a little while before the Tylenol took hold. She began to look on the washstand for the cap to the pill bottle but it didn't seem to be around. There was the ball of cotton that had sealed it, but when she picked it up it was crossed with narrow brown stains. That would be a little more of Sid's doing, Marian thought, frowning. She'd no-ticed the cotton before, hadn't she, and it wasn't just déjà vu. It had not really been a good idea to let Sid into the house. Or Crystal. Or any of that crew. She flicked the cotton ball away and went shivering back to the bedroom.

Her bedside lamp was too startlingly bright when she turned it on. She twisted the gooseneck and set the shade against the wall, and in the faint remaining glow began to search the bedside table and an area around it. No luck. On the floor she began to come upon shards of a wine glass, which she scooped into one place. A fragment cut her finger and she got up on the edge of the bed and licked it. Her free hand, idly wandering, grazed something small and hard just under the hem of the pillowcase and she worked it free. How had it got there, anyway? She cast about briefly for the vanity mirror and gave up. There was only about one good hit left anyhow. She dumped it all into the cap of the vial and sucked it up with a hard snort. A sharp thrusting pain accompanied this action, but after a moment there came the numbness and then the whole headache shrank and began to recede.

Marian caught the last few grains left in the cap on a dampened fingertip and rubbed them slowly into her gums. An artificial narcotic energy began to drive at the very base of her head. From a mass of clothing near the foot of the bed she withdrew a cream-colored camisole and ducked into it. She stood up and walked to another pile, discovered a pair of black jeans, and dragged them up over her hips. With her arms crossed over her chest she spun around twice and then fell backward onto the bed. Her knees came up and she lowered her face toward them and rolled over on her side.

After a time she put forth a hand and drew back a corner of the curtain. The weather outside seemed bright and fair. A greening had come. It must be spring. With the curtain lifted the noise of the street became more horribly insistent and Marian let it fall and rolled away to the inner edge of the bed. The itchiness of mind that had plagued her through the night now returned in altered form. Her tongue was working and writhing in her mouth, and it was hard to hold herself back from grinding her teeth. She got up and went down the hall to the studio.

After the first instant of surprise she realized or remembered that she had to have done it all herself. The studio had a little lock on its door and she had never permitted the more doubtful guests inside. She stood on the threshold blinking at the penetrating light from the corner windows. The room was strewn with a sort of confetti made from a great quantity of her drawing paper. Time passed and she crouched and lifted a strip from the floor. A grinning little simian thing glared up at her — something mutated out of the cherry stone, no doubt. All about she could see other, related gnomes scattered through the debris, all the way to the edge of her eyes' focus; possibly it was these creatures who had wrecked the room. She got up and went out and rested for a moment with her back against the shut studio door.

A passage of time. In the rest of the apartment it was comfortingly shadowy. She had evidently drawn all the curtains and blinds at some previous time. It was good, she thought now, she preferred it this way. But now her mouth was really intolerably dry. Water. She went into the living room and stopped, considering how best to find her way among the great heaps of clothing that covered the whole surface of the floor. Lipping over the sill of the kitchen alcove she could see a number of crumpled bags and boxes, some coated

with a sheen of grease. Among these was a half an eggshell
with a yellow crust around the edge. The eggshell appeared
to shift position just as she noticed it. She went to the bathroom and drank a large amount of water from the tap. She
was terribly thirsty but her stomach seemed to have shriv-
eled to the size of a raisin and she couldn't hold much. The
water was very cold and when she straightened up from
drinking it a hint of her headache began to declare itself
again. The telephone was ringing; she thought it had been
for some time.

Somehow she had not noticed earlier how the hallway
floor was also coated with clothes, but now she slipped and
slithered over it all in her haste to reach the phone. She held
the receiver to her ear but said nothing, and presently
Crystal's voice started up inside the earpiece. *Ah, just who I
didn't want to talk to*, Marian thought, her eyes rambling
over the bumps and pocks of the plaster on the nearest wall.
Crystal never required very much in the way of response.
Marian began to notice that the sounds she was making did
not seem to resolve into words, or if they were words, they
belonged to some tongue she did not understand. At first it
was a little frightening, but as Crystal's voice went on and
on without meaning it became as amusing as anything else,
a relief of sorts, in fact.

Marian took the phone away from her ear and placed it
gently on the table and went away, into the living room,
where she took up a position beside the curtained window.
Crystal's voice continued without interruption, a faint buzzing from the hallway. There was no qualitative difference
between it and the noise of the traffic outside, though from
where she stood the traffic sounded louder. She did not know

how long she stood there, scarcely breathing. At last she went back and picked up the receiver again. The ribbon of Crystal's voice was still unwinding, still devoid of the least significance. Marian hung up.

Then the pain leapt up in her head, bursting open with no real warning, for all she'd been expecting it all day. Her foresight had failed to show her how bad it would be. It revolved jaggedly behind her eyeballs and just under all the bones of her face. Marian mashed her hands against her head, an action which did not lessen the pain at all but only changed the pitch of it. Peering through her fingers, she stumbled into the living room, where she collapsed under the window and rocked her head back against the radiator.

The pain was such a distraction she could not even think in words. Everything else came to a dead stop. Then eventually the pain was very slightly less and her eyes came open again. Fanned out from her and all over the room, the detritus of the past few weeks was pinned to the floor under the weight of its own inertia. What part of it she could not see she could well imagine. Out beyond the curtains the city screamed and screamed. Time obstinately refused to go forward.

How was she to get through this day? And after that another day. And in between the gibbering white night. Impossible. But it was really all the same day after all, the same hour even. The identical moment, suffocating in its awful unity. *No*, she thought, *this can't be. But if I could only get rid of this headache* . . .

She was standing before the blank shelves of the medicine cabinet, empty except for Q-tips and a bottle of corn remover. Naturally Sid and the others would have wiped out everything that could possibly be any good. Her head sank down between her shoulders. She braced herself on the two sides of the sink and looked down into the drain. Then a memory dully woke — she had anticipated this. She had put all the bottles in a bag and hidden it somewhere. It was a yellow plastic bag with black printing on it. What did it say? Her mind ground. The bag was in the pocket of her bathrobe.

By the time she was through not finding the bathrobe she had forgotten that she was looking for it. The search had taken her down other routes. She emptied out what was left in all the closets and raked aimlessly through the stuff on all the floors, even in the studio, and ended by tumbling through old cartons she had not been near for years. When her energy played out she wandered into the living room and saw a swatch of blue velour hanging from under a corner of the couch. It was something she had wanted, she could call that much back through the consuming pain in her head. She drew the bathrobe forth and draped it around her, pulling the fabric tight against the ridges of her body. The lump in the pocket struck against her hip.

She sat cross-legged in the middle of her bed with the robe draped loosely over her shoulders. One by one she took the bottles out of the bag and laid them out among the bed-clothes. It was all there, and there was a lot to choose from. Marian tried to recall just what she'd taken that morning but the information evaded her and its importance began to diminish. She opened one of the bottles and tipped it over; creamy capsules scattered and rolled along the wrinkles of the sheet. There was ample possibility. She opened another bottle and let the pills drop out. The headache was as bad as ever but she knew she'd beat it now.

Then at last she was calmed enough to lie back on her pillow. There was a slow delicious loosening of every ligament and tendon in her body, a tenderness spreading through. Then a sort of weird tingling set up on the surface of her skin. It was as though the mountain of sand that had buried her was being removed grain by grain by thousands of white birds. As she became lighter and lighter the feeling of it became unbearably intense and she could not contain it and she felt she must tell someone at once what she was discovering.

Rising, she felt no contact with the floor; she seemed to hover in the midst of the space of the room, but although the walls were pulsing a little it was easy enough to move forward. It startled her to find that the hallway was empty. She had expected to meet someone there, though she could not recall just who it was she had expected. But the absence was not distressing; on reflection it really made no difference at all. She floated forward, in the direction of the door. Then gravity reasserted itself and she was falling, seeing the hall table flipping over under an unfelt pressure of her outflung hand and the telephone sailing away from the table top and settling in a corner by the door. The pile of clothing on which she lay was airy as a cloud. She began to giggle and for some time could not stop. The spilled telephone chirped and whirred like an insect and Marian was lying in a round field bound at its edges by a cottony substance. Just at the edge of her vision a balloon came wandering across the sky trailing a long, long string through the crisp stalks of dry grass in the field. The string ran undulant like a snake's tail through the grass, lifting as the balloon lifted, so that gradually less and less of it touched the field. The tail end of the string dipped and bobbed, grazing the points of the winter grass, contact attenuating, until it touched the earth nowhere at all. The balloon was higher and smaller and rising more swiftly away and the sky had become less blue, more silver, and the balloon was the same color as the sky.

BEGGARMAN,
THIEF

I SEE IT ALL NOW, Broadway and 106th Street, green trees waving so sweetly to me from that little triangular park while at the same time there's panel trucks scraping into each other trying to wedge into the intersection. I know there's a wino asleep in that park under the fountain and its statue, with that fermented pee smell steaming off of him. In front of that apartment building there's a squad car blinking its little blue light on and off, but I'm away on the other side of the street, over here with the new yuppie shops and the newsstands and the fruit stands and don't forget all those people streaming by all around me, always moving just a little, active and colorful as birds. They twitter and chatter like birds do too, and sometimes it all gets to be a little much and I have to close my eyes and make it all disappear — *whoff* — my whole world gone — a blink and here it comes back again.

It's all in your mind anyway, don't you know?

Though there have been times, places and spaces not always out here on the material plane but sometimes just like in the head, when it has kind of not wanted to return. When eyes closed or eyes open all I can see is a kind of blinking pulsing ball of gray nothing eating up everything there is. The ginch machine, I sometimes call it, which doesn't make it any better or more bearable. It just sits there gobbling stuff, a bit like Pac-Man only with less personality. Very unpleasant, I assure you, but it has not much at all to do with the subject, which is me standing here thinking about Lady Bird offing herself, if that's what she really did, a story which no one is about to ask me for so I guess I'll just have to tell it to myself. I'm sure there's lots more appropriate people, not just cops and coroners but family and friends and lovers too, who'll tell the stories and remember and, yes, mourn. Stupid and superfluous for me to get involved in it, then, only I have to, not that we knew each other well at all, not to the extent of real names even, but because she was a real person and also treated me like one, which at certain times, in certain circumstances, can be difficult to do.

Of which, an explanation. How I came to this particular vertex of space and time is something I don't usually think about too directly, though often I end up humming that little rhyme to myself, the one with all the professions, you know, *Doctor, lawyer, Indian chief . . . da dee dee dum da,* but what I pretty much am these days is a panhandler. I stand somewhere between here and Columbia, making myself a pitiable spectacle in one way or another, and encourage people to put their dimes and quarters into my hands. Hands which are in considerably better condition than some of my other bodily parts, which can cook and sew, hit surprisingly hard if necessary, juggle a little, and even do magic such as making things disappear from one place and reappear in another.

It has been some distance from there to here. And there was that about Lady Bird, that she seemed to be able to look at me and see through to some of the other places I'd been, even the other people I'd been when I was in them. Empathy, if you want to call it that, or honesty.

The first time I noticed her would have been a year and a half — no, two years — ago, springtime like it is now. I was posted down by the fruit stand there, right beside the outdoor bins, because when people know you've seen them go in with money and come out with armloads of apples and pears and avocados, it has this certain effect. Okay, there I was and it was being an average day so far, about eleven in the morning, and *plop* lands a piece of fruit in my hand, a nectarine, as it turned out to be. With this woman's hand still covering it too.

So naturally I look up along that arm and the queer thing was, she was looking right at me, in the eyes, when the average mark is going to look off to the right or the left or even twist around over his shoulders like an owl, he'll drop that quarter from a foot above your hand, so badly does he not want to think about what the two of you are doing. She wasn't my type, I like sharp features, clean lines, cheekbones, and everything in her face was round, only it all went together just right. She had this heavy black hair fanned out around her face and dark eyes just full of the world and the devil. And it wasn't like she was just dumping a piece of fruit on a panhandler, or even trying to turn the tables back on you by giving food instead of money, like a lot of do-gooders will. It was like I was some special friend of hers she was offering to have the first bite. Then she was gone, walking across the street in these bright blue pedal pushers that were just so cute, and I'm standing there holding that nectarine, which was a good one too, heavy and juicy and sweet. Off she goes, and I'm humming that kids' tune to myself — *Lady Bird, Lady Bird, fly away home* — not for any special reason but that's what I called her ever after, in my mind.

It gave me a good feeling, a notion of being on equal terms with the rest of humanity which I don't often get, that lasted all day and into the night when I went to bed in my room-with-the-bath-on-the-hall above Moonbeam's Cocktail Lounge up there on Lenox Avenue. Yep, I live among niggers and like it too, and you won't be getting any apologies for the language either because anyone who gets called a freak can call a spade a spade. And one of these reasons I like it so much is they don't equivocate about what *I* am.

When it started, this present avatar of my wonderful life, was that one day three or four years back when I got off the Trailways up by the bridge and decided to take a long slow walk downtown, not because I didn't know any better but because I did. It had been a bad day, a bad year even, and I was in the kind of mood that's responsible for those stitch marks above my eyes and the way my nose goes back and forth like a mountain road, little disfigurements that for once I wasn't born with but accomplished pretty much on my own initiative. Only nobody stepped on me — people left me alone the way they will a cripple sometimes — and I didn't get anything but tired and mad, so when I was about walked out I went into the toughest, meanest-looking place nearby, which of course was Moonbeam's.

It seemed a lot more promising in there. There was a lot of bloods around the pinball machines and the tables who looked like they'd been out of work a good while and drinking to fill in the time, which tends to put you in the right frame of mind to stomp somebody. So I hopped up on a bar stool and had a couple to start the venom flowing more freely, and then I gave everybody a taste of my accent, and then I began to make a nuisance of myself generally. Pretty soon one of those terrible hurricane silences fell and in the middle of it there was this big movement in the back, which was Moonbeam himself, who wasn't tending bar that day but lounging around in a booth he'd taken the table out of so there'd be room enough for all of him. Moonbeam had been an all-star wrestler on the TV until he got too old for it, with one of those dumbass ring names they have, and after he retired he'd taken the name of Moonbeam to balance things out, I guess, though it didn't exactly fit him.

I watched him coming, thinking, *Well I have sure enough got the job done this time*, and trying to decide if I was pleased with myself or not. Moonbeam lifted me straight-armed with one hand and shoved me up amongst those funky little blue and red light fixtures on the ceiling. I'm hanging there, waiting to get splashed against the wall or the floor and wondering which it's going to be, when Moonbeam speaks.

"Great God, what have we got here but a cracker dwarf."

That storm center silence went on a minute longer and then the poison drained out of me like water and I started to laugh. And Moonbeam started to laugh. Then I was back on my stool and people were gathered around me and we were all swapping life stories and everybody was buying me drinks. The upshot of it all was that Moonbeam gave me that room upstairs for no obligation really, just to mind the store when he was laid up with the arthritis or trying to keep an eye on his grandson Smiley, sometimes, and to the extent it was possible.

Moonbeam turned out to be a smart man, even a wise man, though I'd always thought wrestlers were meatheads before. He looked at me that first day and saw through to all those twisted places and forgave me for them, not with pity because I couldn't have accepted that but with, I guess, a kind of brotherhood. He knew there's all kinds of ways of being a nigger and a lot of them don't got anything to do with your skin. Moonbeam's a man and he's my friend. But I always had that special soft spot for Lady Bird because not knowing me at all hardly, it seemed *she* saw some place down there where I was straight.

What I am, in official and medical terms, is a hydrocephalic dwarf. None of your perfectly proportioned miniature folks, like Tom Thumb and his buddies. Those are pituitary dwarves, my friend. I've got a head and arms and torso probably all about the same size as yours. But from the hips on down it all starts to get real little. Across a table or a bar or any kind of counter, I'm going to look pretty normal. Standing or walking, well, not quite. Though a lot does depend upon attitude.

During childhood there was what they call a complication. It appeared that some parts of my legs weren't growing at the same slow rate as other parts. Result being that my legs started to bow around toward the small of my back. Very painful, I assure you. And finally my hinder parts curled up to where they looked like that gray sluggish part of a hermit crab he's really got to keep hid away in some kind of shell or other.

Don't think I'm complaining because I'm not. Born into Moonbeam's family, say, and I might still be lying up in some stinking bed with my ankles around my neck by this time, sucking cold grits through a straw, or maybe I'd be dead. But from here on out I was lucky, in a way. I had a family, nice kind people whose hearts I later broke, who were first of all white and secondly rich and well insured. Smart doctors from Boston to Miami probed and twisted and sliced and chopped until at round about the age of fifteen they put me back on my feet again.

This is where the attitude part comes in. This is when I became the overachievingest freak you ever saw. I learned to strut like a banty rooster, to where you might not even notice how my legs were, and woe betide you if you did because I was working with weights and in those days my arms were as big around as lots of people's legs. I placed high in the martial arts division of the Wheelchair Olympics (yes, there is such a thing). I taught my hands to juggle and play instruments and pull rabbits out of hats. Meanwhile, I was so smart in school I won a scholarship to Dartmouth.

O frabjous day! The trouble was that none of it really seemed to make me any taller. After a couple of years watching the tall Aryans head out for the ski slopes with their tall Aryan girlfriends, there was this certain encroachment of ill feeling. Oh, it wasn't their fault they were big and blond and stupid, but by God it wasn't mine either. I majored in philosophy, meaning to court the infinite resignation and so forth. There was a visiting prof who was so messed up he had to dial the phone and write with his feet, which should have made me feel better but didn't. I began to feel like, screw the infinite resignation.

In which mood I became an insurance salesman. Major Medical and Hospital Expense. I'd learned before to go right in there for the eye contact so that people never glanced at my legs. A lot does have to do with how you carry yourself, but that can cut two ways, and when I was doing house calls I learned to drag my feet a little. There'd be that first evasive glance and then, "Oh, don't be embarrassed, lemme tell you all about my personal experience, yabbadabbadippitydoo . . . and Purple Albatross paid for every penny!" You wouldn't believe how fast the marks would pony up. Mainly to get me out of the house, I think.

Then there was the breakdown and the institutionalization. And after that I took up a trade which was supposed to improve my sense of self-worth. I got a job managing this shoe repair shop which was completely staffed with handicapped persons — retards, if you want to get specific. The idea was we would all look at each other and everybody would feel just a little bit better about the deal they'd been cut. And the fact is they were the sweetest, nicest people I've ever known anywhere, not an ounce of malice in ever a one of them. Which doesn't do much at all to explain why I one day mugged the cash register and caught that bus which after some zigs and zags and hither and yon deposited me down here.

Here, man, is where I finally learned to do the Change. It has to be sincere, too, every single time. Coming down to work in the mornings, I conjure it all back — every minute's worth of all those years of stale sheets and TV and pain — till the tendons and muscle groups start to tighten and shrivel practically by themselves, till they bring me back to my knees. And that's how you'll see me, near the fruit stand or the newsstand, a sure subject for your compassion and contempt. Pity me, bastards, if you dare, and presto chango, your wallet's gone.

All that is one reason why whenever anybody gives me a really straight look it tends to stick in my head and why after that first encounter I kept a friendly eye on Lady Bird. In a lot of ways she was worth watching, too. First of all there was just the clothes. She had the most amazing clothes. There was the classy businesslike stuff she would wear on days when she was apparently doing something like working. Going out for the evening, well, I beg you to believe she did dress like a princess of one kind or another. But what she really had was this natural way of looking fantastic in even a T-shirt and jeans she'd thrown on to come across the street for a minute.

That's where she lived was across the street on the eighth floor with windows over Broadway, so once I started paying attention I saw her a couple of times a day. She'd be going off in the morning, lugging her big black portfolio, or at night there'd be a cab, sometimes even a limo, picking her up to go downtown. I'd watch her and the people she hung with too, she had a lot of friends, women as colorful and confident as her and a lot of guys, the whole spectrum from punks to pinstripes.

Well, I'm watching all this from knee level over there by the fruit stand, and she stayed friendly after the nectarine episode, even calling me Jocko, which is my street name, not my real one. She'd stop and pass a remark on the weather or tell me some joke or something. Sometimes she'd hand me another piece of fruit and once in a while some idiot tabloid that under other circumstances we might have shared a laugh over.

Other circumstances . . . I'd stay on post till nine or so, long enough to work the dinner crowd, and then duck walk around the corner and up a block to a little bar where I can Change Back. Unlike Superman, I don't need a phone booth; I do it in a revolving door. The door whirls and flashes like a kaleidoscope and I stretch, expand, release — and walk into the bar on my hind legs like a man. Well, what would she have said if she'd seen that? Not much, probably, but she was about the only person I ever wondered that about. I'd vault up on a bar stool and have my one drink, Bombay and bitters, very British, and for ten or twelve minutes I'd let myself imagine I was just killing time prior to dropping in on her and the rest of the gang over there, and then I'd pay and cruise on up to Moonbeam's.

It was a harmless little fantasy, sort of a stand-in for hope, don't you know.

The second spring, a little while after the pomegranate diet, things began to slide downhill. The pomegranate diet was when she ate just one of them a day. I was there enough hours to know she wasn't doing any other shopping. She'd march across the street, buy that one lumpy piece of fruit, march back. Now in spite of my cultivated background I had never actually eaten a pomegranate, so one day I bought one for a lark and broke it open right there on the street. Oh man, all that vermilion complexity.

Meanwhile, Lady Bird was losing weight which she couldn't spare too much of, and after she quit with the pomegranates it appeared to me she progressed to the authentic Beverly Hills diet: stop eating and start doing coke. The composition of the social circle changed too, there got to be a lot of these reedy-looking girls and guys, très chic to be sure but also with that special hollowed-out look of the college-educated junkie. This went on for months and months. The next big thing that happened was she broke up with the guy that seemed to be her primary boyfriend. I remember that because it came at the end of one of the very worst days, the day Benton and Braxton got Smiley.

Smiley and I had an arrangement which was after I had picked a carcass he would run it up and over to a little man who could dump the leather and move the plastic. This went on with Moonbeam's approval, of course. The risk was acceptable, since Smiley was only about thirteen then and clean and on a first offense he'd never even do detention. I loved Smiley in those days. He was like the incredible elongated man, all arms and legs that grew a little more each day, and that amazing smile that bought him his street name, dancing all over his face like a fire. And talented, talented hands. I taught him prestidigitation and up at Moonbeam's, to amuse the bloods, he could make an ordinary Kleenex float and hover like a dove. Also, my friends, he could cajole various items out of your pockets when you didn't even think he was standing near you.

I warned him plenty of times about Benton and Braxton, who were the area squad car, not bad guys for cops, really, but a bit on the humorless side, as cops on duty tend to be. The first time, when Smiley lifted Benton's ticket book, it was at least a little funny. Later when he showed up with Braxton's handcuffs, I couldn't really laugh. But Smiley got hooked on the little adrenal high of it all, and he couldn't seem to quit no matter how many times I told him he'd end up pounded to pulp with at best a civil rights suit for his epitaph.

Then, of course, comes the lousy day when I hear this yelp across the street and Benton, interrupted from pulling paper on an out-of-state car, has got hold of Smiley by the wrist. I can read Benton's mind like it was a thought balloon and he is thinking about how the law can't touch Smiley with a ten-foot pole and then just before I can get my eyes shut good — kee*rack*, he pops Smiley like a bull whip and I can feel it in my own bones that Smiley's elbow has just turned to slush.

On the way to the hospital, I tried to talk philosophy. Whatever doesn't kill you makes you stronger, and like that. A person who's had a long run of good luck will get to think he's entitled to it, only, like the Scripture says, *we are not promised tomorrow*. Look at the advantages, Smiley, I said. You've got a nifty new way to predict the weather now, plus a helpful little reminder from God that the devil is out there too.

But none of it did a bit of good, of course. All he could think of was the good right arm, gone, suppleness and flexibility of it, gone. All he learned was how to hate deep and forever. When he got out of the hospital people had to go back to calling him by his plain old real name of Bobby. This Bobby is just one more terrible thing waiting to happen, anticipating the moment when he can punch a big enough hole in the world to take a few other people out with him.

I reported all this to Moonbeam, who at least didn't hold it against me personally, and then I went back on the job. Nothing else to do but go get drunk and who knows where that would have ended up on such a bad day. It was about six when I got back and I had almost fifteen minutes of relative peace when across the way the door pops open and out flies this guy who was Lady Bird's principal squeeze. He seemed like not a bad guy, either, somewhat too good looking for my taste but with at least a few creases in his face that implied he'd had some thoughts and feelings occasionally. Now he was beating it down the sidewalk like somebody had took a hot poker to him, and Lady Bird was out on her fire escape screaming and yelling things that made even my old jaded blood run cold.

Well, if bad things have to happen they might as well happen all on the same day, and things looked up for me after that, though for Lady Bird, not really. Next morning she came over to the fruit stand, well and truly screwed up for once, for the first time not just her clothes but even the parts of her face hadn't quite fallen together somehow.

She had a five-dollar bill clutched in her hand which it seemed like she didn't recall exactly what it was, and she stopped in front of the bins and stared at them like maybe they were the bars of a jail, about ten minutes' worth of that long dead stare. Then she turned around to me and looked over my shoulder like a regular mark and dropped that five dollars on me. Strung out or not, that was something she was not supposed to do to me so I did something I was not supposed to do to her, which was dip into her purse and lift her keys.

This was an impulse move, I did it without thinking, and when I examined my motives later I still didn't know what they were. But for whatever reason I went and made myself a set of spares before she drifted back from wherever she wandered off to next and I gave the originals back with some line like maybe I saw her drop them. Didn't fool her, I don't think, she gave me a look like she knew who she was talking to, so we were pals again.

It's been around three months from that day to this, none of them terrifically good ones. At first there was this big overt pulling of herself together. Every morning, boom boom boom, off she'd tramp with the portfolio, wearing the business garb. And back she'd come around midday or later and go up to the apartment. There'd be a work light burning up there usually until the time of evening when I split. Not much nighttime going out and next to no visitors. No loitering around the fruit stand either, just a brush by with a choppy wave and a tight little smile that said *later*.

This didn't last and when it quit, it quit with a bang. What was next was frenetic entertainment. Lots of visitors. Parties in the apartment. Taxi cabs. Limos. Very late nights. It was nice to see the girl around the fruit stand again anyway, though as this phase wore on she bought less and less actual fruit. But almost every morning she'd come across, most often with a beer bottle or later with a plastic glass of what I'd guess was vodka in her hand, not that she ever let it show in her carriage. She'd hang out sometimes as long as half an hour, cracking jokes, and she did have a way with a joke. It was the most I ever saw of her, I guess, and she looked great those days (though she was losing weight again), never better, glowing like there was a light turned all the way up inside of her somewhere. Meanwhile, morning was getting later and later until for her it came around five or six at night, and I knew she'd become one of the ones that only light up in the hours of darkness.

From there it was gradual. The quality of her company kind of declined, less girls, more guys, less pinstripes, more punks, until there was nobody left at all but the junkie types. She was thinner, not quite concentration-camp status but *too thin*, and getting puffy around the eyes. And not at all so humorous and lively anymore.

Then she stopped going out. There were still some visitors, the junkie types, which I got to truly hate seeing them show up. Nothing was coming out, but things were still going in, deliveries from like Zabar's at first, then later Chinese or pizza or anyway something.

Then, nothing.

No more deliveries. The hours I put in on the block, I knew. Of course I made an effort at not knowing it. She could have been receiving pizza in the very wee hours of the morning. She could have skipped town under cover of darkness. Two days went by with no action, then three. Those would have been the days she lay up there contemplating her own personal ginch machine or its equivalent. On the morning of the fourth day I discovered what I'd made those keys for and went in.

It was a good-sized apartment, a two-bedroom. Pretty plush for a New York single nowadays. I'd say she had her own money. All the rooms were trashed, but each one in its own special way. In the kitchen it was pizza boxes and Zabar's bags. Roaches galore, I assure you. The corner bedroom, the one with the best daylight, had been rigged as a studio with a drafting table and so forth. That was a mess too, with ribbons of paper all over the place. What she seemed to be into was these frantic obsessive little pen-and-ink drawings, but I didn't have the heart to look at them for long.

Everywhere else it was clothes. You couldn't even find the floor. All her incredible clothes strewn two feet deep, like she just really *couldn't* decide what to wear one day, along that whole continuum of color and form. Oh, there were books and magazines and bibelots stirred into it here and there, but the main thing was the amazing layers of clothes. That and the little fairy ring of empty pill bottles around the bed: Elavil, Valium, Thorazine, Quaaludes, every goddamn thing. We were dealing with a very relaxed person here.

Lady Bird's real name turned out to be Marian, which I discovered from looking in her purse, and she was lying in the doorway from the bedroom to the hall. The telephone had been dumped off its little hall stand and her right arm was stretched out in that direction, not like she was reaching for it but maybe just to point out how silly it was for it to be lying there saying *cheepicheepcheep* like phones off the hook always do. I sat down on a mound of clothes and looked at her a while.

Well, there was that arm, flesh melted all the way back to bone, and yet it remained a beautiful thing. You could see through the alabaster transparency of the skin to the nets of muscle and tendon and imagine how well it all worked when it was alive. And sprawled out in the doorway as she was, it looked like a position she'd chosen, and her face was relaxed, calm, satisfied, for all you could practically see through it to the skull. Easy enough for me to imagine what it would have been like, the ginch machine hovering through all those rooms, sucking away at everything: the furniture, the walls, the floor. Or maybe, since everybody is at least a little different, she saw something else in there when she looked inside, some dreadfully racked homunculus maybe, that feels the way I look, so that whatever she would have been trying to kill wasn't herself but it.

A reasonable enterprise, in its way. Sometimes, I thought, sitting there on the floor, when somebody really wants to depart there's not that much you can do to detain them. All you can really do is hold the door open in a nice way, make your bow, and say goodbye. That's what I was thinking when I finally noticed that little *whoopwhoopwhoop* of a siren that's only half serious.

B-and-E raps are not my style so after a quick dusting down of the doorknobs, man, I left. Only the elevator was already coming open there on the hall, so I had to make my move in the direction of the stairs. I was in Change Back mode at the time and that no doubt is what saved my bacon. It was a long, long way down that hall to the stairwell and it wasn't going to work out well if I ran.

"Hey, innat Jocko?" Braxton says to Benton.

"Naw it int," Benton says to Braxton. "Jocko's a crip, remember, he couldn't walk that fast in a million years."

I love cops, see, because they always know everything. With cops you always arrive at a place where everything can be understood.

Well, safe on the other side of the street, watching the lazy flash of those dome lights, I've changed my mind, which is my privilege. I've had a serious shock, you understand, and everything keeps going in and out of phase: flash, I see it — flash, I don't. Oh, it'll level out eventually. It's all a matter of will power really, and I still have the will. But now I say, *No goddammit you didn't have adequate justification you had no right at all to leave while I still have to stay.* All you've accomplished is to make it a little harder to keep the world in its place, harder for everybody else and especially me. Not impossible, you won't catch me saying that yet, but just a little bit harder, every damned day forward from today.

FEAST
OF THE
ASSUMPTION

IT WAS CURIOUSLY CHILLY and dank in the little bar, which had a cold clammy smell of old beer. They'd put the air conditioning on too early, Sinclair would have said. He'd felt the need of something to warm him up for the occasion, but now the first taste of his whiskey made him shudder too and he had a sip of beer to chase it. He was sitting at the corner of the bar, near a small plate-glass window almost completely curtained by a row of potted plants. Through the gaps between their leaves and vines Sinclair could see patches of the sunlit sidewalk. Outside it was beginning to get warm, the first warm weather of that spring. Inside it was very dim.

The counter top was cluttered with one thing and another: napkin dispensers, condiments, stacks of ashtrays and coasters. Nearest Sinclair was a basket of hard-boiled eggs on which someone had lettered with a Magic Marker the words BONELESS CHICKEN DINNER. *Cute.* Sinclair grinned, then caught a glimpse of the expression in the mirror across the bar and erased it from his face. It was an old-fashioned kind of hole in the wall, but it seemed to have its wrinkles. Still, it looked to Sinclair like the kind of place a person could stay for a while if he had the time. Broad placards hung above the bar mirror announced the price of each brand of liquor in bold red figures outlined in black. The prices were a little high for the ambience, Sinclair thought; also every bottle was outfitted with a bulb-shaped fixed-measurement gadget, a distinct disadvantage. But he was off his beat and had no way of knowing what the neighborhood standard was. Maybe it was because it was so close to Columbia that it seemed a little pricey. He hadn't picked the place deliberately, had just happened to notice it, coming up the stairs from the subway, at around the same time he'd realized he was almost an hour early for the service. You never knew how long it might take to get uptown, but it looked like he'd been overcautious. Sinclair investigated his wallet and ordered another beer.

He was the only customer in the place except for one couple at the far end of the bar. They were distinctly peculiar looking, Sinclair decided, both of them, at least on second glance. The man was noticeably short, with his head freshly shaved, and shining as if it had recently been polished with floor wax, but what really made him look especially odd was that his eyebrows were also bald. The heavy-rimmed glasses he wore gave him a molelike aspect. The glasses were dark and Sinclair could not be sure which way the man was looking; he shifted his own eyes to the mirror, not wanting his attention to be noticed.

But the mole-man seemed completely intent on whatever it was the woman was saying to him. Her hair, brilliant red and with the metallic gleam of too much henna, swirled upward to a point — like a Dairy Dip ice cream cone, Sinclair thought — except that it stood at a forty-five degree angle to her head and seemed actually to be pulling it off balance, backward. But that last part was an illusion, of course. It was her manner of speaking that gave you that impression; she lunged with her lower jaw on every other word, as if she were taking bites out of the underside of something. Her lipstick formed a violet bow whose shape had nothing at all to do with the actual expression of her mouth. Sinclair watched her mouth move in the mirror; he could not make out anything she was saying, but somehow her reflection held him, unwillingly fascinated, by some sense of familiarity which he could not quite resolve. The feeling hung on after the couple paid and left the bar, and did not completely dissipate until Sinclair checked the clock and decided it was time that he left too.

Just inside the nave of Saint John the Divine an area had been blocked off for the service; thirty or forty squat wooden chairs were arranged in a semicircle, facing a row of candles fixed on head-high brass sconces. The rest of the church was unlit except for a single spot on the cross, far back in the apse. The curved rows of chairs seemed isolated, contained by the hemisphere of candlelight. The chairs were all still empty, for Sinclair had managed to arrive too early after all. He went back out into the narthex, where the huge cathedral doors were open and there was plenty of daylight. Just inside the door he spotted Gwen; somehow he'd missed seeing her on the way in. She was in a group of eight or ten people he didn't recognize, and he did not go over. Weber was not among them. Sinclair went out and sat on the top step to wait for him.

It had suddenly turned much cooler and also clouded over completely; no doubt that was why it had seemed so dark inside the church. A cold humid breeze swept across the face of the cathedral, turning back the leaves on a line of trees that stood to the left of the rank of steps leading up to the doors. It was tricky spring weather, Sinclair thought, wondering if it would rain. Every so often people passed him going up into the church, singly or in small groups. Those few that he recognized Sinclair nodded to or waved at.

A woman in a navy sleeveless jumper, with a curious cone-shaped hairdo, was approaching the church from the south. When she turned and began to climb the steps, Sinclair saw that she was the same woman from the bar, although the mole-man was not with her now. Again he was plagued by the feeling that he ought to know her. By the time she had stopped on the step just below him it seemed that her name was almost on his tongue.

"Well, Jimmy Sinclair," she said, cocking her hands on her hips, looking up at him. "Well, don't be such a stranger."

"Crystal," Sinclair said. The name came out of him with the sort of relief that a bursting boil might provide. "I never recognized you, in the bar I mean, I'm sorry. It must be your hair."

"I'll try not to hold it against you," Crystal said. "It's new, the hair is." She smiled, revealing flecks of lipstick on her teeth. Sinclair noticed now that she was wearing fingerless black gloves. An odd ensemble, altogether.

"It certainly is . . . something else," Sinclair said. "Quite a transformation." He remembered perfectly well who she was now, and how he had always disliked her. One of the least attractive of Marian's hangers-on. She was looking at him with a sort of expectancy now, the outline of her lipstick conveying one mood and the shape of her mouth another.

"Such a shame about Marian, don't you think?" Crystal said at length.

"Yes," Sinclair said.

"And what it's going to do to poor *Gwen*, I just don't know, she always *depended* on Marian so."

What a crock, Sinclair thought. He had not known either woman well, but he'd always thought that Gwen was the more substantial of the two, and she was the one he'd always wanted to know better.

"She's inside," he said, after a short awkward pause. "Gwen is. Inside the church."

"Coming in?" Crystal said.

"In a minute," Sinclair said. On the sidewalk below he could see Weber approaching.

"Well, then . . ." Crystal let her hand flop forward on her wrist, a wave of sorts, and climbed past him toward the entrance of the church.

Weber was now coming up the stairs. He wore a long dull green raincoat buttoned to the throat, hanging in a smooth fall from his neck to his ankles. Sinclair stood up to meet him. The raincoat made Weber seem strangely disembodied. Facing him, Sinclair opened his mouth to speak, but no word would emerge. Weber's eyes were hooded, ringed with black; he looked as if he'd had no sleep for days. Sinclair reached out and set the flat of his hand against Weber's collarbone, feeling the life there. There was a rumbling that might have been either a subway or thunder far away. Sinclair cleared his throat.

"It's all right," Weber said, lifting a hand and touching Sinclair's elbow from below. "Let's just go on in."

It was not going to be a funeral. The body had been shipped back to Chicago for burial, an orthodox Catholic ceremony; that had been the week before. This service was only a memorial, an opportunity for Marian's local friends to gather. There would be, it appeared, a reading of psalms. The first person who stood up to read was unknown to Sinclair and he found that his mind was wandering. He had not been much in church since childhood and the rhythm of religious language tended to bring back the old childish torpid inattention.

He began glancing half surreptitiously around the area from his place in the second row. There was a fair showing, thirty or thirty-five people. Sinclair did not recognize very many of them, and those he did know he knew only by name or face, for the most part. He had not really moved much in Marian's group, only occasionally, because of Weber, who now stood up from his place beside Sinclair and went forward to replace the person who had been reading before the row of sconces.

"*My soul is full of trouble,*" Weber said. "*My life draweth nigh unto the grave.*

"*I am counted as one of them that go down into the pit, and I am even as a man that hath no strength;*

"*Cast off among the dead, like unto them that are slain, and lie in the grave, who are out of remembrance, and are cut away from thy hand . . .*"

Sinclair flinched. Weber's voice was all wrong, too harsh, too outraged. His raincoat was still fastened completely shut and in the candlelight it resembled a ceremonial smock or robe. He was, Sinclair realized, reciting the psalm from memory.

"*Thou hast laid me in the lowest pit, in a place of darkness, and in the deep . . .*" Weber's shadow stretched out, dark and wedge-shaped, into the circle of chairs. "*I am so fast in prison that I cannot get forth.*

"*My sight faileth for very trouble, Lord; I have called daily upon thee; I have stretched forth my hands unto thee.*

"*Dost thou show wonders among the dead? or shall the dead rise up again, and praise thee?*

"*Shall thy loving kindness be showed in the grave? or thy faithfulness in destruction?*"

This was not reconciliation, Sinclair realized; it was not coming to terms. Weber's voice grated with anger, and Sinclair could not guess where it was directed, whether at the whole assembly or at Marian, who had deserted him, or at a god in whom he did not believe. Whatever the target, it was alarming enough. A nervous rustling set up among the rows of chairs.

"*I am in misery, and like unto him that is at the point to die: even from my youth up, thy terrors have I suffered with a troubled mind.*

"*Thy wrathful displeasure goeth over me, and the fear of thee hath undone me.*

"*They came around me daily like water, and compassed me together on every side.*

"*My lovers and friends hast thou put away from me, and hid mine acquaintance out of my sight.*"

Weber stepped forward. For a moment Sinclair thought

that he was actually falling, but he was only turning to drop into a chair in the front row. On the whole Sinclair was relieved that Weber had not resumed his place next to him. The next reader was a woman he did not know. Her voice was neutral, calming. All around the area there were little shifting sounds of readjustment.

Sinclair found it easy not to listen. He sat back in his chair, cautiously, and looked up into the vaults of the ceiling. The glass of the windows held a little light but none of it seemed to filter down. Sinclair wondered whether it was really raining now. He lowered his head and glanced up at the speaker, then around the front row. Weber sat at one end, stooped over with his chin resting on his hands; he seemed to be looking past the speaker, into the light of the sconces. There were several empty places to his right, a gap through which Sinclair could see the others sitting in the front row, all unknown to him but Gwen, who was sitting at the opposite end.

There, it seemed, was a natural place for him to rest his eyes. Gwen was in profile to him, with her hair on the near side pulled behind her ear. She wore a plain white collarless shirt. Her face was turned a little toward the speaker, and Sinclair could see her eyes shining with reflected candlelight. All the parts of her face were smooth, not featureless, but with one feature blending into another without lines of distinction, a movement that couldn't be described. In the candlelight, Sinclair thought, she looked like a La Tour Madonna. Then he recognized that the feeling in him was desire, and, ashamed of that, he turned away and closed his eyes.

Marian. She had not been much like Gwen, Sinclair didn't think, though they were closely related and had been good friends. Marian had even resembled Gwen somewhat, detail by detail, but the sum of the parts was completely different. Marian was all nervous edges, had none of the deep tranquillity Sinclair associated with Gwen without having any real way of knowing whether it was really there. The truth was that he had always been uncomfortable with Marian, she had always made him jumpy in some way. He had not loved her. Perhaps she had not been easy to love. But Weber had loved her and he did love Weber. In this context there was nothing else to call it, and so there was a chain that went from him through Weber to her, and possibly, through her, to others too.

Silently, Sinclair began a rote repetition of the Lord's Prayer, word by word, trying to concentrate. He made an effort to summon a whole image of Marian before his mind's eye, but found that he could not do it. The picture of her that he brought before him disintegrated, its interior broken up by light. The light was like that of the sun or of stars, and Sinclair saw that his picture of Marian was being drawn up into it, consumed. But that was not the word, it was *assumption*. The Assumption. Sinclair twitched. It was the wrong association; Marian had been no madonna. Still, that image of her persisted, a vague human outline flooded by a powerful inner light.

Unnerved, Sinclair opened his eyes. Gwen was standing in front of the candles now, reading from a small black-bound psalter. Her head was tilted a little over the book and her hair, falling forward, obscured her face. Her voice came out of her with a clear measured gentleness.

"Lord, let me know mine end, and the number of my days, that I may be certified how long I have to live.

"Behold, thou hast made my days as it were a span long,

*and mine age is even as nothing in respect of thee; and verily
every man living is altogether vanity.*

"*For man walketh in a vain shadow, and disquieteth himself in vain; he heapeth up riches and cannot tell who shall
gather them.*

"*And now, Lord, what is my hope?*"

Gwen looked up, out over the ranks of chairs. There was
a charged pause, which Sinclair found a bit disturbing.
Gwen glanced down at the book, then back at the assembly,
and now spoke even more slowly.

"*For I am a stranger with thee, and a sojourner, as all my
fathers were.*

"*O spare me a little, that I may recover my strength, before I go hence, and be no more seen.*"

It had rained, in fact, but only a little. The portico and the
steps of the cathedral were spattered with droplets here and
there. The sky was clearing now, though it remained cool
and breezy. To Sinclair the day seemed much brighter than
it had been. The mourners grouped on the portico were
speaking among themselves more loudly than they had been
on arrival, and every so often Sinclair heard someone laugh.
He himself felt rather relieved now that the ceremony was
over. Weber, he noticed, was standing alone, hands in his
coat pockets, staring out across the street from the middle
of the portico. Sinclair walked over to him.

"Well," he said. "What's on the program now?"

Weber turned and before Sinclair had any opportunity
to read his expression his foot came lashing up out of the
folds of his raincoat. The foot was shod with a black cloth
slipper and the edge of it looked as sharp and heavy as a
hatchet blade. Sinclair blocked the kick and retreated, sink-

ing reflexively into a back stance. The habits were clicking automatically into place; it might have been regular Friday practice with Weber, except that it wasn't. The energy of Weber's next kick popped two buttons off his raincoat. Sinclair heard them ticking away across the portico, but he couldn't afford to let his eyes chase them. He would have liked to get a look at Weber's face, too, but it was essential to stay focused on his hips and shoulders to read the next attack: another side kick. Sinclair blocked hard, with plenty of follow-through, hoping to swing Weber off balance, but it didn't work. The next kick was already coming and Sinclair almost lost his balance backing over the door sill into the narthex. He had worn his good shoes for the occasion and the slick leather soles made for poor traction on the polished floor. The light from the doorway glared in his eyes now, a further disadvantage. He had room for about one more step back, then contact would become a serious issue. When he felt the side of his foot graze the wall behind him Sinclair screamed, a barking sound forced sharply out of him by a clench of the diaphragm. The vaults of the church interior trebled the yell, startling even him.

Weber dropped his stance and stood there all undone, hands shaking, eyes loose in the sockets.

"No kidding," Sinclair said. He straightened up too, but slipped a little to one side, so that the light was more favorable and he had clearance to back into if necessary. He could see that a cluster of people had formed in the doorway, watching them, both Crystal and Gwen included.

"Yeah," Weber said, passing a jittery hand across his face. "I'm sorry, man, I don't . . . I think I better get out of here."

"Definitely," Sinclair said. "Maybe I'll go with you?"

"No," Weber said. "No, I'll be okay, you don't have to."

"I wouldn't mind."

"I tell you what, I'll call you tonight," Weber said. "Around eight, I should be home. Don't worry, I won't be doing anything unusual."

Sinclair reached out and flicked his shoulder, as if for verification.

"You swear?" he said.

"Sure," Weber said, and grinned shortly. "We thank you for your patience."

"Any time," Sinclair said. "I'll try you around eight."

"Oh, I'll be there," Weber said, and with a thumbs-up gesture he turned and started for the door. The tails of his raincoat, which was torn completely open now, fanned out behind him. The people in the doorway parted rather quickly to let him through. Some shaded their eyes to look after him; among others, conversations were resumed.

Sinclair stretched his hand out in front of him, pleased to see that although he seemed to feel it trembling there was no visible sign of it. He began to walk forward, slowly, toward the doorway. There was a disjointed sensation back of his knees, but he felt that his pace was steady enough. Crystal had turned to Gwen and was speaking to her, apparently picking something up from where it had been dropped.

". . . but she was always such a *destructive* person, really, so it really shouldn't come as such a —" Crystal sat down suddenly and put her hand to the side of her face. As if in hindsight Sinclair saw how Gwen had swung her purse backhanded, choked up so tight on the straps it must have been almost like striking with the flat side of a board. *Criminy*, Sinclair said to himself, *the girl's got talent*. He had come up beside her without breaking his gait and now, not thinking anything about it, he slipped his arm through the bend of her elbow and carried her quite naturally along with him down the steps.

"Well, it's quiet," Sinclair said, turning his hand palm-up and spreading it as if to point out the stacked coasters, the cruets, the boneless chicken dinner. There was no trade at all in the bar now except for the two of them, and the bartender was wrapped up in a Walkman at the end of the counter, communicating by hand signals only. "It's pretty quiet in here."

"It picks up a little at night," Gwen said. "Students. A lot of students come."

"I figured," Sinclair said. "Seemed like that kind of thing."

"Marian used to come here in the daytime some," Gwen said. "She liked it . . . She liked how dead it was. Relaxing." She picked up her glass and looked at the ice cubes.

"Well," Sinclair said.

"Sorry," Gwen said. "It's just that almost everything around here reminds me of her now."

"Ah," Sinclair said. "You're about to get the classic cop-out. I don't really know what to say."

"Oh, that's fine," Gwen said. "You're nice." She looked up at him as if surprised to find him there. "I don't really know you."

"Not yet," Sinclair said, and couldn't believe he'd said that, right after a funeral too. His heart was pounding, aghast at the nerve of him, exactly like some fifteen-year-old's heart. Gwen lowered her eyes and traced a circle on the counter with her fingertip.

"I'm a little embarrassed, you know," she said. "Back there. I'm not like that. I just . . . I lost control."

"There seems to be a lot of that going around," Sinclair said.

"True," Gwen said. "We've had quite a day of it, between us." She looked back at him curiously. "Could you have stopped him if he hadn't quit?"

"I don't know," Sinclair said. "Not if he was having a good day."

"Well, what do you think got into him?" Gwen smiled. "As far as that goes, what do you think got into me?"

To his own considerable surprise, Sinclair felt that he actually did know the answer to this question. But he couldn't quite think of the right way to phrase it.

"Everybody must have been a little jumpy, under the circumstances," he said. But no, that wasn't it at all, he'd lost it now. "Maybe it was just a little cloud of craziness passing over . . ."

"Maybe," Gwen said. "Well, thanks for the drink. I kind of needed it."

"I'd buy you drinks all night," Sinclair said, thinking, *Shoot the moon.*

"No, I'd better go," she said. "I need to try to mend some fences. That was a bit of a sudden departure there."

"Of course," Sinclair said. He looked at their two hands, crooked toward each other on the counter top; another inch, two inches, they'd be touching. "I realize it's really not the time." Feeling that Gwen was watching him, he glanced up. A sudden burst of light from the window turned her left eye from gray to green. Sinclair held the gaze, thinking she must be seeing through him to the bone.

"We'll be in touch," she finally said. "Weber would know how to reach me."

"You know I'll do it," Sinclair said.

"I know," she said. "You will."

Then she had slipped down from her stool and was out

the door before Sinclair even had a chance to stand up for her. He felt an impulse to follow, but restrained it. A cloud must have passed away from the sun, for now light poured in the window, through the vines, flooding Sinclair's corner like a liquid. It was wrong, completely inappropriate, but he felt very happy, couldn't remember when he'd felt so good; it was like coming out of hibernation. He raised his hand and flexed its fingers in the sunlight, wondering at the intricacy of their movement. *Why, it's just that we're still alive,* he thought, regaining the words of the answer now. *That's all that's wrong with us.*

AS WE
ARE NOW

N*o.*

I could just put the phone down. Drop the receiver on the mattress beside me, watch it bounce and settle back. Lie down and listen to that voice trickling out and puddling on the sheet. No sense, no words even, just some sort of metronomic ticking, a new way of reminding oneself of the passage of time. The beauty of it is that she never would know. I could even, if I had the energy, throw on some clothes and trot up to 13th Street and buy a bag and come back with it without her ever knowing I was gone. Or I could just sit here and hold the receiver in my lap and stroke it like it was a kitten.

No, Crystal, I am definitely not listening to you.

There is always something in her conversation that sort of inspires detachment. I'll be sitting right here with the phone to my ear even, possibly, and my mind will just float off and hover in the middle of the room, poised between the one-two drip of the bathroom faucet, and the buzz and whine of her voice in the phone, and the grind of the traffic across Rivington Street under the window. Or any other three points you might care to name.

The mind just tends to wander. Goes tripping and stumbling down its own foggy pathways. Away from something that isn't just a hangover but a deep bone sickness, through to the marrow. Away from the point that it's morning, or I've woken up, at any rate, away from the point of the telephone. I can let it ring and ring and ring but around the fifteenth ring I know it's Crystal and I know she'll never stop. I'll lie turned away from it with my head tucked under the pillow until the mattress turns into a slab of rock and the pillow turns into an anvil with that ring slamming into it like a series of sledgehammer blows.

Good morning, Merry Sunshine. It's little Crystal calling.

well, what are we going to do today, hey, what are we going to do today, hey, what are we going to do today, *hey*, what're we gonna do today, *hey*, what are we gonna do today, *HEY*, what are we . . .

Sometimes, up around the hover point, the head can get stuck in one of those little patterns. Maybe it's Crystal's conversation that brings it on, but I've always suspected that it's really its own little independent thing. It can be very difficult to break the chain once it gets started. And the worst thing about it is that it doesn't stay exactly the same.

It keeps shifting just a little bit, in some detail or other, going in and out of phase. The principle of Oriental torture, as I understand it.

". . . you know, Sid, sometimes I think I might be turning into some terrible total mental case . . ."

Yes, every now and then, despite all defenses against it, a couple of lines do leak through. Like skip on the radio band, or something. Now you hear it, now you don't . . . But it is a bit disturbing when it connects like that, to whatever it is you happened to be thinking. Even though I know it's got to be a complete accident every time. Crystal's conversations are so repetitive, such a tight loop, that it really would be just about impossible to tell one from another, even if you were trying to.

Still, it can be a bit unnerving. When it hits a nerve.

Unnerving when it hits a nerve. Unnerving when it hits a nerve. Unnerving when it hits a nerve unnerving when it hits a nerve unnerving when it —

Sometimes, with a major effort of will power, I can cut it off. Can roll over, stuff the telephone inside the pillowcase, smother that tick-tock voice almost completely. Almost. Not quite.

The truth is, it just doesn't do to actually hang up on Crystal. That is the one thing that gets her really angry. The one humiliation that's almost bad enough to stop her coming back for more. Oh yes, it really makes her mad, and she has her ways of letting you know about it, somewhere down the line. And meanwhile, although she is a very tiresome conversationalist, she does have her usefulness. Every other call or so she really is on to something. Something really good, or cheap, or otherwise out of the ordinary. Something worthwhile. And over time I've learned to catch those clues without really listening for them at all. I can just pick them out of the jungle of her talk, like Hansel and Gretel homing in on the famous bread crumbs, following them all the way home.

Oh my God, but I am sick today. What have I got? Have I got something? If my mind falters on that question, it usually means the answer isn't good.

". . . I mean can you *imagine* it? Actual physical *violence?* And Gwen? *Gwen!* Why, I mean I never would have thought she had it in her . . ."

Now where have I just been? It seems I've been taking a little vacation here. Looks like the phone has snuggled up against my ear again somehow.

Next question is, have I got any money?

Once, way back almost before the dawn of time, I knew a guy who was an ex-junkie. Two years off the stuff he was, but he said he was still on the run from it. A foreigner, French, German, Italian, Rumanian. Something, anyway. His English was a little unorthodox, that's all I really remember now. But I remember talking to him one time, oh, way back there, in a café. One of those little pseudo-European cappuccino shops on MacDougal Street or somewhere, with tables out on the street and all. It was just a few days after I'd had my very first little sniff of the big number. Oh, it was nothing much, just a little flutter, a flirtation, one dance around the pit with the dark angel. But it was much on my mind. So that I wanted to talk about it. Not only to impress and frighten people either, people who hadn't had even that one short dance. Though it was fun to do that too. But I wanted to talk about it to someone who had been there. Someone who would *understand*.

And he did, this guy, he really did understand.

He was smiling the whole time we were talking about it, a kind of nervous slippery smile. Hands fastened around a glass coffee cup on a white ironwork table. It was a sunny day, as I recall, so bright it almost hurt. "Oh yes, but so much," he kept saying, smiling the whole time and understanding perfectly, I could tell, "so much you have to have at last, only to be as we are now." He kept saying that over and over, rephrasing it only slightly, smiling and shrugging his shoulders, the smile running around and around his face, as if he could still taste it.

I knew he was absolutely right, of course. That much was as plain as the nose on your face. Still, I didn't feel connected. Not yet. Like, *What does that have to do with me? I never put a needle in my arm.* Oh, the fecklessness of youth. Actually it wasn't really all that long ago.

Only to be as we are now . . .

And the next question is, can I *get* any money?

". . . you know, as if any of *them* had been looking after her . . ."

Not much in the way of authentic signal in Crystal's rap today, nothing that I can pick up on at all. Can't quite make out what she's talking about, but I can tell it's definitely not the right thing. No help there, nope, not today. No hope. Nothing. Sometimes that's enough to make you lose your composure. I might catch myself with my hands on either end of the receiver, just about ready to snap it in half. Like I really can't stand that voice trolling along for as much as another second. However, I've just got to be patient, because I need my little Crystal. Dear little pilot fish that she is.

Now there's a comet tearing across the ceiling way high up there above the mattress. A face of some kind in the ball of it, flesh blown back to the bone with its speed, mostly skull. With a long raggedy tail of fire trailing out behind it. Interesting, isn't it? Gives me a little shiver, too.

Though actually, the truth is, it's just a rough patch in the plaster. It's got a way of looking like different kinds of things. First one and then another. I can get stuck looking at it, for hours at a time it sometimes seems. Especially on a bad day. One of those can't-get-up days, I'll just stare and stare at that blob of plaster, waiting to see what it's going to do next. Funny how it works. It'll be just nothing for the longest time. Then, *whoa, whoosh*, death's head comet. And much as I might try to stare it down, it'll just keep on being that and being that and being that. Like one of those two-way reversed-field drawings that can get jammed in one mode, just won't flip over. Then, when you give up altogether, start to look away, it finally changes.

I've got to think.

There. I saw it move. An actual crack opening up along the side of that patch. That really happened. Or no. No, that crack was definitely there yesterday. Last week? Or maybe it was always there. But the whole thing's done it, anyway. Now it's a dog, a big wedge-headed dog, asleep with its shovel-nose tucked under a paw.

".. . and isn't that just too pathetic for *words* . . ."

Back to square one. That's the worst of Crystal's monologues. One of those stray phrases will sneak through to derail your train of thought, just when it looked like it might actually go somewhere.

Where was I, oh yes. The Problem. Now, let's concentrate.

Assuming negative answers to those first few questions, what I need now is a friend. Or an acquaintance. Not any one so cooked as Crystal. I need someone a little underdone. Someone close enough to the edge, but who hasn't been over that often yet. Someone ripe for a little flutter. A dance or two on the rim. Who'd appreciate a pick-up, wouldn't care to have to cop their own. With money to spare and enough not to watch it too carefully.

Yes, there's something a little queasy about the whole idea. There is, I know it. But. But.

". . . and the way *he* was acting, I could scarcely describe it, really it was just the freakiest scene . . ."

Dammit. Concentrate.

To be as we are now . . .

Now. Where do we find this person?
Daylight. Couldn't pin it down past that, but it's definitely

daylight. I can tell that much from the volume of the traffic and the color of the light in the room. Which is really just too bad. Because the ideal thing would be a party, or a club. But it's obviously too early for anything like that. Nothing shaking.

Oh dammit, Crystal, you've got to run out of gas soon.

So it's got to be somebody I already know. Who's had a flutter or two already, preferably. Someone it would be okay to just call up in the middle of the afternoon, *say, what about* — Susan? Bart? Marian?

Marian.

Marian is ripe. Marian is ready. Marian has been walking the edge like the edge was a tightrope. Marian has reached the position from which the next move can be anywhere. Marian could do anything. The crux. Vaguely, vaguely, I can remember being there myself.

As we are now.

Marian. I think I'm in love. I just call Marian, get the go-ahead. I know I can get it if I do it right. Then . . . the dance of the thousand phone calls. Oh, just a few thousand phone calls to get it all set up in a nice way. And then, finally, we're home free.

Okay, two minutes to work up the charm.

Now, one minute to curtain. Show time!

Only, dammit, the line's busy. Not hers, of course, but mine. Crystal's got extra staying power today, or so it seems. Is it possible I could just cut her off? Nope, not a good idea. She'd smell it. She has her instincts too, the little darling. Patience, patience is required.

But, with an object distinctly in view, I can be very patient. I can wait for a very long time indeed, so long as I know it's coming. Patient as the grave.

Oh, get on with it, Crystal, for God's sake.

". . . but can you feature them all acting that way? So *possessive*. As if they were the only ones that ever had any interest in her at all. It was practically . . . *ghoulish*. Really, that's what you'd have to call it. It really was ghoulish. Such a way to behave at a funeral too, or a memorial, or whatever it was supposed —"

and now I've got panic slavering all over me like nightmare movie effects and I can't even tell why why why Marian's dead she's dead she's dead she's dead as a freaking nail and *how long have I known it?*

Well. So much for that. So much for that, anyway. Good Lord. Good golly. Good golly Miss Molly. Good golly Miss Molly. Good golly Miss Molly. Good golly Miss Molly. Good golly Miss Molly. Good golly Miss Molly. Good golly Miss Molly. Goodgollymiss. *Oh yeah.*

I remember I heard about it and I. I heard it was an OD. *Slam bang*, I thought my heart was going to blow blood out my eyeballs it was going so fast and hard and I was thinking, *How, how could it have been that, she never would even touch a needle, for chrissake.* Trying to think back, how it could have happened, remember everything that happened, the last time I was up there, I couldn't even remember when that was, because what if it somehow all came back on me? Yeah, what if they somehow hung it all on me?

Now *when was all that?* Well, Crystal knows. But hey,

wait a minute, the phone's hung up. Now how did that happen? Either she hung up or I did, I suppose. Not to worry.

Where was I? Yeah, that's what's been odd. That's what I must have been listening to. That funny little humming silence that comes around the back of that voice whenever it stops. That little eerie drone you seem to keep on hearing whenever Crystal finally, finally shuts up.

But where oh yes. Sometimes. Sometimes all times seem like the same time. Right here right now, wedged in one long consuming moment, with the daylight switch stuck on, forever's worth of a single second of a single afternoon. Just me and The Problem here. *As we are now.* Oh let's not start.

A hawk or a buzzard possibly comes down through the ceiling, wings folding in a stoop, plummeting toward my face. Green, green rushing up at me, so fast I can't tell what it is, and then I level out and glide. Trees. A big grove of broad-leaved trees with the leaves washed upside down in the hard wind, pale undersides of them flickering side to side. I was in the park, I was in Tompkins Square when I made the call, could that have been just yesterday?

No. I'm not listening.

Marian was dead and I was scared. I was scared because I couldn't remember exactly what but I was scared and I was sitting on a bench after the first call, cold all through, and I was thinking. Is there a hell, is she there now? Or is it maybe that I'm there and she's gone out?

Now just walk through it. I can tell now if I just walk through it there's got to be something waiting at the end.

Well I got up from the bench and went and copped and then.

Then it was dark and I was in the park again. Windy, still blowing the trees all around and I was in the phone booth and I had that feeling the wind can make on your face, like something's been rubbing it a long time, a soft cloth. And that was when I made the other call. To Crystal, yeah, I called Crystal, and she told me what, it'd been a week already, and she told me it was pills.

Pills. Kind of a stupid thing to let happen to you, if you ask me. Still, so far as I'm concerned, no problem. Nothing personally involving me. A shame, of course, but no direct effect.

But just keep walking.

And then I. Then I checked my wallet. And there was still enough for two more bags. One for tonight. One for *tomorrow.*

It's tomorrow. I swear it's tomorrow. I've arrived.

So it would have to be in my pants pocket. Rolled up at the foot of the mattress, I'm sure I just now saw them there when I was going after the phone. Little Crystal piloted me into something after all, didn't she? In a way she did, at least. Because otherwise I know I never would have rolled them up like that. It's there. I know, I know, I'm almost sure it's there, in a minute I'll sit up, and then I'll have it.

THE
HOMELESS
DEAD

You MIGHT THINK being in a wheelchair you're too slow to catch up with things, the world passing you by and all that. But I see it more like the other way around, you get going too fast and you miss everything. That's if Robbie is pushing the thing, at least. That's why I'd rather use the walker in the end.

Now you know I wouldn't seriously complain about Robbie, wouldn't do it for the world. He's my grand-nephew and it's his first year in NYU and it's more than most his age would do to give a part of a Saturday or Sunday over to trolling a dried-up crippled old lady around lower Manhattan in a wheelchair. Really, Robbie is just as nice as pie, always has the nicest smile, like the man in the moon, though I've been tempted to wonder if anything much goes on behind it. Robbie and I don't really *communicate*, as people like to call it on the TV. It just would not make sense to him if I was to ask him, for instance, why he has to move so goddamn fast. Where does he think he's going to get to sooner? Hell itself, or just the grave? No, but if I asked Robbie anything like that he would start to think I was senile or crazy and pretty soon other people would start thinking that same thing. Then I would be jerked out of my nice little rent-controlled apartment on Waverly Place and slapped in a nursing home about as fast as you can say the words, something my daughter would like to see happen because she's worried about my welfare, and my landlord, too, because he's worried about his.

So it's *How's your schoolwork, Robbie*, and *S'all right I guess, Aunt Marie*, and *Don't study too hard now, Robbie*, and on and on like that. Boring, really. But it is fresh air.

It was last weekend, Robbie had taken me out and it was shake, rattle and roll across the park and down to the Grand Union, where I wanted him to run in and pick me up some cottage cheese and corn plasters and things. Across the street on the block above the store the man who collects for the homeless was there. I know him well by sight. He sits behind a little card table with his hands folded over each other behind that enormous green jug people put their money into. I set him as a target when I come down on my walker, the weeks he's there. Some weeks he isn't. No matter how long it takes me to get to him, I've never seen him move a hair. He doesn't seem to need to shift around, not any more than a snake would. His face is the color and texture a brick might have if it had been underwater for about a thousand years, and has the same expression. Drinking did that, I wouldn't wonder, and yet he seems a steady man. I believe that he must know me too. Finally, at long last, I'll come up beside that table and I'll sling a quarter into the cloudy green glass lip of the jug and hear it ring on the other coins inside. You can't imagine how it makes me feel, a real accomplishment, like I had all of a sudden turned into Kareem Abdul-Jabbar and started making slam dunks. Then the man always gives me some sign of recognition. Not a round of applause, not a nod or a wink. Maybe it's just a dilation of his eye, but he somehow manages to give me some sign that he knows just what I've done.

Last weekend there was something new about his set-up, only from across the street I couldn't quite make out what it was. Eyes not much good anymore, along with everything else. All I could see was a big black square with white something on it. Robbie parked me at the end of the bicycle rack (a wonder he didn't chain me to it too) and took my little list inside. I sat there and thought it over. You get as old as I am and everything's a political decision. I tried the question out in my head to see if it sounded crazy, and decided I could get away with it.

"Let's go back up the other side of the street, Robbie."

"Sure, okay, Aunt Marie."

Only of course we were rolling along so quick I didn't have much time to take it in, plus the sidewalks were crowded with the weekend traffic, so I didn't really get much of a clear look. I could just see it was a big black bulletin board with white squares of paper tacked to it, but I couldn't see what was on them. At the top in big block letters like a movie marquee it said, THE HOMELESS DEAD. Well, even that little was enough to start me thinking — feeling, I should say. Those white squares against the black looked so much like a graveyard that when I blinked my eyes I was looking across the slopes and the tombstone files of Arlington again, where they buried some bits and pieces of what they claimed was Robbie's grandfather back at the end of the Second World War. I opened my mouth to tell Robbie what I was thinking about, and maybe even get him to wheel me back for a better look, but that would have sounded like dwelling on the past or something, of course.

"Pretty day, isn't it, Robbie?"

"Yes'm, it sure is, Aunt Marie." It was, too, one of the first really good days of the spring.

Back home I sat there and felt bad the whole rest of the day. I kept seeing that bulletin board cemetery and trying to match it to different other things in my head. What exactly was bothering me I couldn't have told you, it was like it was just around a corner, just barely out of sight, and that frightened me good, the way it always does these days. Because someday what disappears around that corner could be something as simple and necessary as my own name. From the cradle to the grave the body is in a race with the mind and now what I pray for is that my body will get there first. *Please*, goes that little prayer, *don't let it be some mental thing, and don't let it be something just incapacitating either. Let it be something major, like my heart.*

The picture of that bulletin board and the words on it had got to me somehow, and I kept thinking about it all through the week. When Saturday came around again I decided I just had to go back and give it a better look. If I saw exactly what it really was, I believed I might get rid of the thought of it. It would have seemed like such a crotchet that I didn't want to ask Robbie to wheel me down there. I might have dreamed up some kind of excuse, but I finally thought I'd prefer to go by myself.

I wake up long before most people do, except for other old ladies, I guess. That Saturday morning I had luck and the elevator was working. Without it I wouldn't have had a hope in hell of getting the walker down the stairs. When I came to the street it was barely good light yet and of course no one was around. That's the only time of the day the city's truly quiet. I started heaving the walker in the direction of the park.

What's that like? Well, imagine that you were so decrepit and done in that you had to throw your whole weight on a stone wall just to hold yourself up. Then imagine you had to pick up that same wall at the same time. Then think about covering some distance that way. Of course there's no real risk of feeling rushed. In fact, you'll have generous time to memorize every blasted stalk of grass and every crack in the pavement.

It was warm weather so I hadn't needed to put much on, nothing but a raggedy old cotton dress, you could just about see right through it. I left vanity behind me a long time ago, and fear along with it, for that matter. I didn't have a purse or even a pocket. It's not so bad to be helpless, really, the trick is you've got to be worthless too.

By the time I had hauled my sack of skin and bones to the bottom of the park it was quite some time later and there were a few more people around. Since I've been slowed down so thoroughly, it's begun to astonish me how other people can move, like water spiders flashing from one place to another without your really being able to see how they do it. Whereas I must have looked like some kind of inchworm, humping myself over to the corner of La Guardia Place where I could see all the way down to the grocery store.

He wasn't there. Sometimes he isn't, like I said. Of course it was awful early. I kept going down toward the place where he usually sits, picking up the walker and slamming it back. I won't deny I was disappointed. After every step I managed to make I looked again at the spot he should have been at, like I thought maybe the sidewalk was going to open and pop him out, table and jug and bulletin board and all. But naturally when I finally did get there the spot was just as empty as it had been all along.

I stood there and rested and blew awhile. The sun had come all the way up and I was getting kind of warm. Still, I thought I'd go on. There was a little Italian place I liked, just a few blocks over to the east, and this time I had better luck and it was open.

Actually it seemed a little funny for a bar to be open that time of the day. It must have been all of eight o'clock by the time I got there. I think it's that the owner gets lonely, or maybe he just can't sleep in the mornings, same as me. I'd call him a young man but he must be in his sixties, a solid Italian-looking face on him with all the parts of it rounded like a water-smoothed stone. He doesn't get the morning drinkers, not like an Irish bar. There's a little coffee pot he keeps going and he puts out a basket of rolls and pastries I think he probably just buys retail at the bakery up the block. Probably throws most of them out in the end too because he doesn't get much trade. Me sometimes, but I don't eat, and now and then some other stray. There was one young couple that used to be kind of regular, a boy and a girl who would come in for a light breakfast sometimes, still warm and sleepy smelling from the bed.

It was pleasant to come into the cool dim, out of the glare of the sun. I nodded to the owner, who was sitting all the way at the end of the bar by the window, and started toward my table in the back next to the phone. There was a hiss and a clink and I knew he had opened me a beer, though I had my eyes fixed on the black and white tiles of the floor. It pleased me the way he did it without being asked. By the time I got myself lowered into the chair he was at the edge of the table with the squatty brown bottle and the short little glass. I unscrewed one of the caps from the walker and pulled my ten-dollar bill out of the tubing. Always makes him smile to see that, and I think it's pretty slick myself. He took the money and rang it up and carried me back my change. It's a courtesy, they don't normally wait tables here, but he can see how I'm fixed and I'm not about to turn it down.

I sat there for a nice long time just watching the cold vapors curl out of the mouth of the bottle, because, you see, I had to make it last. I can't afford to drink a whole beer, not that I don't want to. All I can have is one glassful, I guess about six ounces. The rest I just leave on the table. The owner could wash his hair with it, maybe, if he had any hair to wash. The trouble's not in my head, it's with my kidneys. As I found out one very unpleasant day, if I drink the whole bottle I don't make it back to the apartment. That's old age for you, and you can have it. You will have it too, if you survive; that's what survival's all about.

On the other hand, if I could drink a whole beer or maybe a bunch of them I might turn into the old lady who sits in the bar all day long and plays "Mack the Knife" over and over and cries. Then you wake up one day and you've been taken out of your own hands and your last little bit of freedom is gone.

If that nice young couple happened to be there, I could

offer them the bottom half of the beer. The boy didn't drink it but the girl wasn't above a little beer with her breakfast. That's how I got to know something about them. The boy was a schoolteacher and the girl said she was some kind of artist, I think. They weren't married, of course, but I was way past worrying over that.

There was a bar of light creeping across the floor as the sun moved, and I waited for it to touch my chair leg before I poured out my glass of beer. I raised the glass and sort of ate a little of the foam. After I had waited some more time I let myself have a good swallow. Then I finished the glass fast enough to get a really strong tingle out of it. Since it was all I was going to get I'd learned how to make it feel good. That tingle was just beginning to fade when the schoolteacher boy walked in the door.

"Over here," I said, not thinking. I was just pleased and relieved somebody had turned up for me to offer the rest of the beer to. I wasn't sure he'd recognize me but he did. He smiled and came over and actually sat down. Then he looked like he wasn't sure what was next. We'd never really talked a lot, not more than a word or two in passing.

"Got half a beer for you here," I said. "I was just pulling myself together to leave." My thought was to let him off whatever hook he might think he was on. His hand came halfway toward the bottle and stopped and I saw something cross his face, like a memory had come back to him he'd just as soon had stayed away. I wondered, did he have a little spat with the girlfriend? and then some devil got into me and started flapping my mouth.

"Now what's become of that girl you go with? *She's* the one takes morning beer, now I recall."

You would have thought I had hit him with a lead pipe

between the eyes. His face got a look like a blank sheet of paper.

"She died," he said, looking over my shoulder. "Killed herself, that is."

Something went out in me like a candle, and I wished real bad I'd stayed home. Before I knew it my hand went out and closed over the boy's wrist, which felt about as lively as a stick of wood.

"That's terrible, son, that's just terrible." It sounded like the exact right word when it came out, I think it was the *terror* part that convinced me. It was a piece of what had been puzzling me all week, I thought, but now I was sorry I had it.

"I know it is," the boy said. "But I'm not sure she did it on purpose."

That's when I actually saw my hand on his arm and I thought, *Oh no, what do you think you are doing? You go around putting your old skeleton hands on practical strangers, and you know where you're going to end up.*

"Excuse me, I'm sorry," I said, meaning about my hand, which I took back and used to stuff my money back into the walker. Then I heaved myself up and started clanking toward the door. I don't think the boy noticed much, he seemed a long way gone. I don't suppose I'd made his day either, not exactly.

It had got cloudy outside all of a sudden and the sky looked like the sole of somebody's shoe coming down. I felt terrible, terrible, terrible, and I wished I'd never come out. What I needed was to see something good, something that would make it worth the trip. It didn't have to be a big thing necessarily, but a freaking flower wasn't going to do it.

There was nothing. I'd hoped the man with the money

jug might have turned up, but he didn't. By the time I got
back to where he would have been I was about nine-tenths
worn out. It was late in the morning now and people were
either jostling me or wishing me ill under their breath when
they got stuck behind me and had to slow down. The
weather had turned so muggy my hands were slippery on
the frame of the walker and sweat ran stinging down my
every crease and wrinkle underneath my clothes.

It was peculiar, but even though the streets were getting
crowded there was hardly anybody at all in the park when
I finally got there. With the overcast it looked all gray and
dull and not like anywhere you'd much want to be. A
woman with wires stuck to her head was hopping up and
down in front of a tree with a horrible jerky motion, like
she was being electrocuted. She hung there in the middle of
my sight, twitching. By this time I was so tired out that a
pulse of red light had started up behind my eyes, and I really
didn't think I could raise the walker for another step.

Where I came to a stop was beside some benches and I
stood there propped on the walker, trying to make up my
mind if the relief I would get from sitting down would be
worth the effort it would take to get up again. I was staring
over the back of the row of benches, across an empty stretch
of scraggly grass. A chunky young woman and a little boy
met each other just where I was looking, both of them as
dull and shabby as the grass was. They nodded to each other
with some kind of complicity, and each took a long step
back. The woman lowered herself on a bent knee, her arms
swung up slowly from behind her back, and out of her
hands a bright red ball appeared, floating on a long flat
curve into the raised hands of the boy. They each took another backward step and the boy's hands dropped and rose

with a scooping motion and the ball flew out in a longer swoop to vanish into the woman's loosened sleeves. Again they stepped back, on an easy rhythm, and when the ball reappeared in the air between them I knew that I was seeing what I had wanted to see. My spirit rose back up inside me like a wave. *Thank you, thank you,* I said, not caring for the moment if it was out loud or not. *Thank you so much for that little good feeling.* Actually I'm not at all convinced that there is anybody to thank, but somehow it always feels better if I can make it personal.

Whatever the reason, everything jagged in my mind was dropping smoothly into place. I shut my eyes a second and the white squares on the black board returned to my memory, and it came to me so simply what I'd missed about that phrase. I had been thinking of it as two things, when all along it was just one thing. Everyone fears to be homeless, I've feared it myself a long time, but what is it finally but to be let out of the old bag of flesh we all drag around like a snail its shell? My heart began to race with the thrill of seeing that little truth. *A little truth —* The rest of the sentence got away from me, turning the corner. I opened my eyes and squinted my mind, trying to catch hold of it. The woman and the boy were still lengthening the distance between them, the ball still linking them together with the pace of a heartbeat. *Will set —* I saw the ball vanish and return — *set —* the ball stopped in the air like the dot on a question mark — *set me free.*

WORLD
WITHOUT END

IT WAS THE RAIN that made her decision final. A tap, a blink, and it began to spatter all down the gray length of 14th Street, a cold greasy rain, all wrong for spring. It made everything seem even more insupportable than it had before. Gwen had brought no umbrella and she hurried toward the corner of Sixth. It was dark enough that she could see through the plate-glass window of the coffee shop without being seen. Sinclair bulked in a booth toward the back, waiting because she had kept him waiting. She went in ordinarily as if all were well and joined him.

"Wet?" Sinclair said. His hand covered hers where she had carelessly left it exposed on the table.

"Not too," she said. A waiter appeared with the two heavy plastic-sheathed menus, a good pretext for her to retrieve her hand. She hid inside the menu for a couple of minutes. There was a lot of food to be had, after all, and suddenly she was ravenous. Her stomach clenched and did a flip; then she solved the terrible difficulty of choice by choosing quickly: eggs and home fries, corned beef hash. Comfort food.

The waiter came and went, removing the shield of the menu. Gwen remembered what she'd thought on the drizzling street, *No putting it off this time*, and regretted it a little, looking at Sinclair. Though he was almost completely bald, just a few lonely sprigs of reddish hair scattered across the top of his head, he wasn't bad looking at all. He had a strong face with friendly creases around his mouth and eyes, which were a light, transparent blue. *He'd been good in bed too*, Gwen thought, *too bad about all that*, and realized she'd never be able to touch the food she'd ordered.

"I can't," she said. Sinclair's eyebrows cocked. Gwen lowered her head and turned it so that a fall of her pale hair came over one of her eyes. "I don't think . . . I'm not hungry at all, not really," she said, rushing and beginning to mumble too. "Maybe just some coffee?"

"Had a bad day, have you?" Sinclair's tone was even, noncommittal, but Gwen knew this sort of thing infuriated him. She kept her face averted toward the puffy vinyl padding of the booth. Sinclair got up, slapping the flat of his hands on the table top.

"I guess I'd better stop the waiter."

Gwen listened to the sound of his feet going away and kept on watching the patina of dirt on the red leatherette. She knew how he hated to interfere with waiters. Being served by anyone made him nervous and apologetic, even in a coffee shop. Things were getting off to a grand start.

"Coffee's coming." Sinclair was back and Gwen turned and tossed her hair back out of her eyes. Did he get it?

"What's up, Gwendolyn?" His tone remained studiedly neutral. "What gives?"

He'd know, of course, that these sudden reversals of decision meant he was in for a rocky evening at the very least.

"It's no go," she said.

"What's no go?" said Sinclair. But she could tell he did understand her now. It was a relief of some sort to have the subject declared, or not quite relief but that point-of-no-return headiness that one might feel, say, at the top of a ski slope. The one time Gwen had actually skied she'd gone hurtling down with a total lack of grace and skill into a damp white whirling, and later they were telling her how lucky it was she'd only sprained her knee. She dismissed the memory now; it wasn't a good precedent.

"What do I get if I argue?" Sinclair said.

"Failure."

"Thought I might," he said with a half smile.

"Well," Gwen said. The waiter set down her coffee and she warmed her hands on the side of the cup. "It's hard to make this kind of conversation very original. I don't really know what to say anyway."

"Want me to guess?" Sinclair said. He did sound a little edgy now. "Ah . . . it's not working out. Things we do together are getting a little boring and maybe it's us and not them. We fight too much about things that shouldn't matter and we can't make up like we used to. We care for each other but not enough to overcome anything. Couldn't really call it love, could you? You can't make up your mind about much of anything lately — you can't make up your mind to stay in this, so you think you'd better get out. We're both a year older than we were when it started and it's not going anywhere much and you need to find — ah, scratch that. Let's just say you're ready to be alone now for a while."

Sinclair reached for his coffee and slopped it all over his hand.

"Dammit," he said. "Am I close enough?" He dried his hands and put them over his face and held them there for a moment. When he took them away his eyes were very tired.

"I'm sorry," he said. "Didn't mean to be nasty."

"You weren't," Gwen said, choking a bit. She hadn't planned on that. "Honestly, Jimmy, you don't have anything to be sorry for. Only it's just — well, you see how it is."

"Yes," Sinclair said. "I do. But you used me. You did use me."

Gwen sighed.

"You always let me," she said.

"I know." Sinclair rattled his blunt fingertips along the Formica table top and let them settle. "Well, there we are."

"Friends?" Gwen said.

"Better give me a little time on that one," Sinclair said, sounding really peevish for the first time. "I was a little bit in love with you, I think, back there for a while."

"Oh, dammit, Jimmy, I'm sorry . . ." Gwen said. "I mean probably I was too."

"Of course friends," Sinclair said, smoothing the table's surface with his palms. "Call me in a week or so. Lunch, whatever. When you want."

"Thanks, then," Gwen said. "It may be more than I deserve."

Sinclair looked up and smiled at her, a wide easy smile without reservations.

"Oh, I wouldn't say that," he said. "Don't worry about it. Take care of yourself, Gwendolyn. Don't let the bastards get you down."

Outside it was raining harder than before and Gwen bought a cheap folding umbrella at the corner. She chose a lurid floral pattern, to buoy up her mood. Then she crossed to the east side of the street and got on line for the Chemical Bank machine. Because it was supposed to be spring she had worn openwork shoes and now her feet were soaked. The socks were only helping keep the water in. She'd have a hot bath when she got home, that and a lot of red wine and aspirin and a lot of TV. It was completely dark now and the inside of the coffee shop was lit up like a diorama. She could hear the bank machine beeping softly as she shuffled forward in line.

In the coffee shop the waiter was bringing Sinclair a check and he was standing up and putting money down on the table. Gwen watched him sling his jacket over his shoulder and walk toward the double glass doors. When he got outside he paused and looked in her direction, but Gwen did not think he could see her; it was too dark and she would never have owned such a tacky umbrella and he knew she had no account at Chemical Bank. Sinclair shrugged into his jacket and walked a couple of doors down to the narrow front of the Muse Tavern. He would stay there for a long time probably, getting very drunk on beer and whiskey. In the morning he would punish himself for the excess by working out twice as long and hard on whichever martial art it was that he and Weber practiced. Somehow it was cheering to Gwen to be able to predict all that with reasonable confidence. She stepped out of the bank line, pointed the umbrella into the wind, and walked toward Seventh Avenue. The wind swept around in the other direction and the umbrella swelled, pulling her along after it like a sail.

Not having a boyfriend anymore was not a good enough excuse to take a cab, Gwen advised herself, snapping the garish umbrella shut as she went down the steps to the IRT. A slimy puddle had formed on the landing and she skipped over it, starting to run toward the sound of a train moving in the station. But it was a downtown train, and she slowed down at the turnstile. *Walk, don't run.* It was silly but true that having Sinclair had made it a little easier to take the subway whether he was with her or not.

Something she had to start getting used to, wasn't it? This early in the evening the uptown platform was unthreatening enough, not crowded but speckled with reassuring Upper West Side types. Gwen waited near a woman more or less her own age who wore a zebra-striped coat and carried a pink Reminiscence shopping bag, shifting from foot to foot in her squelching shoes.

It took the uptown express only a couple of minutes to come in. There were plenty of people in Gwen's car. She cased them quickly and leaned back, not quite closing her eyes but slitting them. Four years before she'd been snatched into a subway bathroom by a man she could only describe later as big and white, who'd slapped her, thrown her against the wall, and then inexplicably bolted without doing anything else, no rape or robbery. He'd cracked two of her ribs and left her with a deep-seated horror of the subway, and yet to urge herself against that feeling, Gwen had discovered, seemed to reduce her vaguer fears of other, less formed things. She eyed the other passengers through her lashes, with some odd sense of secret power, as the train rushed in and out of its stations.

At the newsstand outside the 72nd Street stop she paused and bought some papers very quickly without looking at them: the *Post*, the *Voice*, *People* magazine. Bathtub reading. The rain had slowed to a sprinkle and she did not need to unfurl the umbrella for the short walk to West End Avenue. One block over and two up, and she had opened the heavy wooden door to her building and was climbing the carpeted stairs.

Key in the door, she froze. *Like a rabbit in headlights*, she thought, hating herself as much as the syndrome. It was the most she could do to turn herself around so that at least she would see if anyone else came up the stairwell. Her key ring pressed a node in the small of her back, from which the paralysis radiated. If she went in now she would sink instantly into a chair, onto the floor maybe, and she might stay there motionless for hours, with no power to run a bath or take off her shoes or make any of the gestures of living.

It wouldn't do. There was no use to go into the apartment like that, but it wasn't good to be nailed to the hallway either; at least inside it was comparatively safe. *Oh, this is absurd*, Gwen thought, hating it all wildly, and then recalled the last thing Sinclair had said: Don't let the bastards get you down. The panic withdrew a little, not leaving her altogether but remaining present without touching her, like the walls of a box, or a room. Ever so slightly she began to relax. It was something to have been loved after all, even unsuccessfully.

All she really needed was a plan. Nothing required her to stay in the apartment, did it? Her weekend bag was completely packed and waiting by the door, ready for the morning departure. *Why not tonight, then? No reason,* Gwen thought, beginning to hope. She could picture the trustworthy canvas grip, its rolled leather handles, placed solidly just within the room. All she would have to do was (1) pick up the bag, (2) call the garage, (3) leave. She faced her door, only a little tremulous now, and turned the key.

Now the rain had completely stopped. Gwen rode a wave of exhilaration up the Henry Hudson Parkway, speeding just a little. How easy it could be to take control of one's life after all! It had been less than a year since she had first learned to drive, when for so long she had thought that she never would. Now she went a little faster, weaving among the other cars, at ease, lifting her eyes every so often to look over at the dark silky sheen of the river, with city lights glittering, suspended down inside it.

She accelerated through the ramp to the bridge, savoring the twist and pull of the turn. At the bridge entrance the traffic thickened and she had to slow down. Gwen shut her eyes a moment against the chain of taillights climbing ahead and opened them again. The inside of the car glowed with confident, practical signal lights, registering everything in running order. From the rearview mirror there hung a little swing on which two plastic lovebirds perched, beak to beak. That was Marian's touch, Marian with her flair for transforming the tacky into something slightly transcendent; she was also responsible for the laminated portrait of Saint Dymphna, glued up under the green glow of the dashboard. And of course the whole car had belonged to Marian too before she —

Well, I just might get rid of all that stuff, Gwen thought, shifting lanes as the cars spread out on the bridge. But really, she didn't need to do that now. The recurring shock of recognizing them had faded, day by day and month by month, turning finally into something else. Remembering Marian was no longer so sharply painful as it had once been. In spite of the fact that Gwen had lost whatever faith she'd been trained to and believed in no god and no afterlife, Marian's disappearance from the world had come to feel more like a separation than an absolute loss. The talismans had lost their power to wound and become a kind of comfort, and memory now was bearable, necessary even. Gwen turned north on the Saw Mill River Parkway, picking up speed; there was quite a long way ahead yet.

Darkness sealed her tightly into the car. The Taconic was pretty driving in daylight but by night it was no more interesting than anything else. When Gwen felt her eyes begin to lock too steadily on the roadway ahead she put out her hand and touched the scanner button on the radio. A station played for twenty seconds, then the next and then the next. It was an irritating gadget, really, more of a nuisance than a help. Nothing on the whole band appealed to Gwen enough for her to stay with it, and when the scanner had run two complete cycles she reached down and turned the radio off.

With this you can forget about decisions, Marian had once said, it fails to make decisions *for* you. Fully auto-

matic . . . Gwen smiled in the dark. It was odd that when
the call had come her first reaction had been to seek her
earliest memory of Marian. It was hard to distinguish what
she'd been told from what she actually remembered, but
what finally had come to her was a sharp sensory apparition
from parochial school: smell of chalk and dry paper, scratching of fat-barreled pencils, the look of her own shiny black
shoes, which fastened securely across the instep with a little
strap. Two desks ahead of her and across the aisle Marian
leaned out to lift, delicately and inch by inch, the veil of
Sister Mary Consuela, who had stopped stock still in one of
the reveries she sometimes fell into, on her way from the
rear of the room to the front.

Sister Mary Consuela . . . that would make it first grade.
There was a current of muffled tittering circling the room,
but Marian never smirked, being too expressionlessly concentrated on her task. Gwen, ever a goody-two-shoes, was
frightened, but acutely interested too, watching the slow
rise of the veil. Surely something terrible would be revealed,
and what emerged was yard after yard of Sister's flat black
habit, enveloping as night. Gwen blinked and pulled the car
back to the crown of the road; it had been drifting toward
the shoulder. Perhaps it had been terrible enough after all:
black on black on black . . . When the old nun finally felt
something and turned around Marian had already vanished
into her polite posture at the desk, feet set primly together
on her chair rung, demurely masked. Devilish as she could
sometimes be she never exposed herself for nothing, never
gave up anything for free.

If not the first memory, that was the first datable one, but
in fact they'd known each other much longer than that, had
even known each other in the womb. A family joke. It had

always charmed Gwen to imagine her mother and her aunt, neither long out of high school, both newly married and hugely pregnant, only a couple or three weeks apart, as it turned out. They'd been inseparable, so the story went, shopping as long as their legs would carry them, escorting each other to the baseball games they both adored, eating absurd, overwhelming meals. And so she and Marian, un-named and half formed, would have been inseparable too, ipso facto, floating in their adjacent orbs of amniotic fluid. Marian, who'd almost always be the leader, had been born first and easily, while Gwen, as she was later told, hadn't seemed to want to leave at all.

Liked it better where I was, no doubt, Gwen said to her-self, mouthing the words. The high beams of a speeding car came up quickly behind her and passed by on the left. Never since had she been quite so at home in the world, not like she always imagined her mother, her aunt, to have been. In the pictures they both looked so young, and in fact Gwen's mother had been only nineteen. Ten years younger than she herself was now, Gwen recognized with a physical wriggle as if she'd been pricked. It had been surprisingly sharp of Sinclair to discover how badly she'd begun to want a child, and kind of him to have snatched the words out of his own mouth . . . A bell-shaped hollow opened inside her, rang once and disappeared. She'd done the right thing. For now.

Of course her mother and her aunt had probably both married blind: two brothers bent on doubling and redou-bling their money and who'd succeeded very well at that, almost beyond dreams of avarice. They'd moved their wives and children out of central Chicago and slowly across the subdivisions and at last to the big houses in Winnetka, from which there was nowhere left to go. That enormous house with its endless, bland appointments, a cocoon that answered every wish or need almost before it could be fully formed, articulated. Impossible to be unhappy there. It had never been heartless luxury, not for anyone involved in it. She and Marian had been well and truly cared for, prized and treasured through and through. But Marian had slit the silken tent to slip out into a harder world, and Gwen, more shyly and with more painful hesitation, had finally followed her through the rent.

It remained a mystery to her, exactly why she'd had to go, but mysterious or not it was absolutely so. Childhood's world turned out to be a backward lobster trap; instead of its exit it concealed its entrance. But inside or outside, Gwen's place had always been nowhere. An outsider would find it hard to understand how so much generosity and love could be so overwhelmingly difficult to survive; it was a ridiculous proposition — but Marian had not survived it. Proof positive. Darkness visible . . . Gwen glanced up from the center line of the highway and briefly met her own eyes, ghostly in the rearview mirror. The last memory followed with illogical ease upon the first, Marian's last surprise in a career of surprising the people who knew her best. Gwen had never, ever thought it would be Marian; she'd always expected, and at times found a kind of solace in the belief, that it would be herself.

Where the Taconic ended Gwen did a short hitch on I-90 and exited onto a northbound secondary. She'd been on the road more than two hours, and it wasn't much farther now, she knew. Things seemed a little unfamiliar in the dark, but she couldn't find the slip of paper with the list of turns, so there was nothing to do but trust herself. Autopilot. At a crossroads she went left on a potholed unlined pavement and drove for a mile, a mile and a half. A graveled drive appeared in the pool of her headlights, and she turned in, feeling the car grind and slip a little on the hill.

The white clapboard house stood halfway up the slope, just ahead of the ridged shadow of the tree line, its dark windows reflecting the headlights back at her. She drove around and parked at the side of the house and carried her bag up the steps to the back porch. No need to lock the car, not here. When she stopped outside the kitchen door she noticed for the first time the soft curtain of sound the tree frogs made. The key was where it was supposed to be, under a bleached white conch shell on the windowsill.

She was the first one up this season, and inside the air was thick and unusual. Gwen groped along the kitchen wall for a moment before she remembered that the light turned on with a pull chain. She circled toward the center of the room, stumbled over something, hit the edge of the table with her hip, and found the cord.

The kitchen was in some disorder, as the rest of the place would probably be too. It always seemed to happen when the house was closed, despite all manner of good intentions on the part of everyone. An array of last year's pots and pans was spread over the gas stove, the sink, and the round central table. Gwen saw that they at least were clean, if a bit dusty, and had only not been put away. A box of kindling by the big wood-burning range had been overturned, possibly by someone's dog, in the wake of a hasty departure. The broken wheeled horse and the tin wagon, one of which she'd probably tripped over in the dark, belonged to Vincent, Annie's four-year-old. Annie would have shoved them into the house along with the rest of Vinny's smaller "summer toys" now scattered across the plain planking, not really knowing where they landed, her mind engaged with some other project, like containing Vinny in the car. Sweet natured but a bit scrambled, that was Annie, but Gwen liked her, found even her vagueness appealing enough. She and Vinny would turn up tomorrow afternoon, though Henry, husband and father, was off on some travel-writing junket and wouldn't be coming with them. Carolyn was coming up, so was Weber, and possibly Tom Larkin. They'd all planned to converge on the house for the first spring week-end sometime on Saturday, but Gwen had beaten them all to it, now.

And beaten them to the mess as well, she thought. Squaring away the wood and the toys would take only a minute, but the range had been belching cold ashes, those dishes had to be rinsed, everything was thick with a winter's worth of dust, the floor needed a mopping, a scrubbing even . . . But not tonight, Gwen decided, suddenly exhausted, the late drive hitting her full in the face; it would all keep till tomorrow, and she might get enough communal points by giving it just a lick and a promise and making the first major run to the store. She locked the door and put the key in her pocket, since she was there alone. The house creaked gently as she moved across the floor to get her bag. She wouldn't even look at the other rooms, not until tomorrow, she told herself as she walked down the shaft of light thrown from the kitchen doorway to the stairs.

Her bedroom was a small one, just wide enough to fit the bed and a small night table beside it, securely close. The air was stale but it cleared quickly once Gwen knocked loose and opened the little sash window that overlooked the road. She made the bed with sheets from the hall closet, then pulled her nightgown out of the bag and undressed quickly in front of the warped mirror tacked to the inside of the door. It was a nice little body, she concluded, irresistibly giving it a cursory inspection, still firm and resilient enough. Her own. The face above it was unconfident, the sad dislocated face of a lost child. Gwen turned her back on it and dove into her nightgown.

Red flannel furled around her from neck to ankles: instant warmth. She tipped across the cold hall floor to the bathroom and hastily washed her face and brushed her teeth. Then she came back and crawled into the bed, wriggling her shoulders against the mattress, anticipating sleep, and turned off the light. The lamp's bulb faded in a succession of sulphurous auras and Gwen snapped wide awake, all of her unease and panic instantly returning. The tree frogs outside went *scritch-scratch* like nails on a chalkboard. It was too much, after she'd really tried to beat it, driven so far to get it all out of her system. What the hell was the matter with her anyway? Annoyance was better than fear and nausea, at any rate. She switched the lamp back on and reached down for the papers she'd bought earlier, shoved into the side pocket of her bag there half under the bed.

Ritual reading of the *Post* had cured her insomnia a few times before. She began with the funny page, then Dear Abby, then the Rigby cartoon. Toward the end of the gossip items on page six she began to feel that reassuring sense of boredom spreading over her like an old blanket, and her eyelids started to droop again. Drowsily she turned the page and there on page eight was a quarter-column picture of Weber in handcuffs, captioned: "Mystery bridge climber didn't mean to jump?"

The story was short and Gwen skimmed it: ". . . Police cajoled . . . said he had no plan to harm self or anyone . . . found to carry no I.D. . . . could be charged with trespass and/or reckless endangerment . . . psychiatric observation . . ." There went Weber's weekend. Was it really him? Yes, no doubt about it. It was his disjointed, half-amused expression that had first caught her eye, a face he might have worn up here, for instance, walking across the field from the creek. Weber looked reflective, rather pleased with himself, and utterly unaware of his surroundings: the stanchions of the bridge, a slice of river, handcuffs, the two policemen flanking him, expressionless as the ones who —

Gwen glanced at the date at the top of the page, slapped the paper down on the covers and jumped out of bed. Who would have thought that a subconscious calendar could be quite so accurate? But sure enough, it was the very day. So that was what had been plaguing her ever since she woke that morning; it was a relief, even a sort of thrill to know. Typical of Weber, whose obsessions always drove right to the surface, to commemorate the first anniversary with some such grandiosely stupid gesture. Gwen stared at the crumpled newspaper on the bed, almost expecting it to move, to levitate. It wasn't panic now, just her mind rushing too furiously forward toward comprehension. She picked up the house key from the dresser and went downstairs, clasping the key in the shallow pocket of her gown.

It had been in her mind to go for a walk, but she was barefoot and it was silly to go wandering around the countryside in nothing but a nightgown. She stopped on the porch and stood with her back to the dirty kitchen. There was a pricking around her eyes, her body wanting to cry, but she had already cried enough on that subject, though of course the mourning, in one form or another, would go on forever. *Well, I do miss you, there's no bones about that,* she thought, knowing that she could not be heard but feeling somehow as if she were. A wave of fatigue swept her forward and she caught herself on the porch rail.

A lean cold moon had risen, shining down over the valley. The surface of the paved road gleamed like a river. Gwen's mind turned itself inside out and she remembered the job of cleaning out Marian's apartment — weeks it had taken. No one had seen her for quite a long time; everyone thought that someone else was seeing her, but she'd assiduously quarreled with them all. The chaos was not frightening in the end, simply amazing, a side effect of a mind that had absolutely stopped caring where it was, if it even knew. Everything had to be examined, for salvage, for value, for some further clue to what had happened, and there were plenty of clues, of course, all leading in different directions. One had struck Gwen hard enough that she'd slipped it into her pocket, a folded business card from some art supply store, and printed on the back in Marian's tiniest, most neurotic writing, a line from Camus: *"Le ver se trouve au coeur de l'homme. C'est là qu'il faut le chercher."*

Gwen squeezed the porch rail, keeping her grip. *Oh, it is there we must look for it, indeed.* She had kept the card for a month or so and then one night, in the clutch of some mood, she had burned it. But of course that made no real difference. One doesn't exorcise the worm so easily as that, not from a heart that will nurture it. Gwen shivered inside her red flannel; the nights up here were still cold. She pushed herself back off the bannister and stood up straight.

On the opposite hill the treetops made a crisp black line, dividing the curve of the land from the sky where the moon drifted. Gwen put her hand on a square post of the porch, not for support but only to feel of it. It was gone, she understood, the worm that had worked at her own entrails for so long. Maybe she had only imagined that it was ever there at all. It must be a rare thing for anyone to really want to die. She'd never know if it had come about for Marian by completion of her will or by some perverse combination of a half wish and chance. The sure thing was that if Marian had not died, she would never have had to learn how to drive that car. At some level it, or what she could make of it, was as stupid and as simple as that. She had never expected to be the stronger one, had not wanted to be, but she was. Now she could feel that terrifying strength running all through her; it would never abandon her, and she would not be able to discard it either, all of the days of her life. Comfort or curse, it was hers for always. She would live for a long time, probably, but now she knew she would not sleep, not tonight, and so she went into the house and found a broom and began to sweep the kitchen floor.